Look for More Titles by Cassandra Chandler

LINGERING TOUCH

Tied up in Customs

The Department of Homeworld Security
Book Four

Cassandra Chandler

Copyright Page

Tied up in Customs
The Department of Homeworld Security, Book Four
Copyright © 2017 by Cassandra Chandler
Print ISBN: 978-1-945702-35-8
Digital ISBN: 978-1-945702-23-5

First eBook edition: June 2017
First print edition: December 2018
10 9 8 7 6 5 4 3 2 1

cassandra-chandler.com
P.O. Box 91
Mission, Kansas 66201

Dedication

For Holly A.—an awesome Earthling.

Don't miss out on any of the alien action.
Subscribe to Cassandra Chandler's newsletter at
cassandra-chandler.com!

Chapter One

"What is Brendan getting me into now?"

Eric mumbled the words under his breath, scanning the diner as he pretended to read his menu. He made a mental note of the access points of the room—doors, windows—possible lines-of-sight for snipers, items that could hide threats. Everything was cataloged.

Booths lined the seating area, and the central space was filled with a maze of tables. He had asked for a spot near the back wall, where he could easily see all the entrances and exits, as well as the patrons and staff.

The diner didn't use tablecloths, which helped his survey. And it wasn't a place he visited often enough that it would be easy for anyone to predict him being there. Brendan had been very specific that he wanted to meet in this place, but had hedged about why. Which meant he was up to something.

Once, he had roped Eric into being part of a zombie walk. Only once.

Even though Brendan had made Eric swear he would be unarmed when they met, he'd still nearly dislocated a civilian's shoulder trying to protect Brendan from what Eric perceived to be an attack. Brendan had thought it would be okay because zombies "weren't real" and Eric "should have known it was just for fun, since it was his day off..."

For a genius, the guy could be an idiot. Much like Eric was starting to feel.

This was going to be another zombie walk. He just knew it. Especially since Brendan had once again made Eric swear to come unarmed. But if that's what it took to get Brendan back to work on the communications array, so be it.

Honestly, Eric kind of thought Brendan's weirdo play-acting games were...fun. Not that he'd ever admit that to anyone.

Eric was looking forward to this entirely too much. Maybe he did need to take more time off. He could even try to find someone who shared his interests.

Let's see, that would be protecting people, maintaining peace, finding a way to improve everyone's standard of living without compromising what each specific country has achieved, understanding that I'm absolutely dedicated to my job...

At least, he used to be.

He and Brendan had been talking about Eric's single-minded dedication to his job way more than an asset and handler should. Eric chalked it up to building a good rapport with Brendan, but they had come dangerously close to crossing into friend territory.

Crap. They were totally friends.

Eric should ask for a reassignment. Hell, maybe he should retire, like Brendan was threatening to. Find a job in the private sector. With the way his superiors were handling Brendan's project, he might even be able to do more good there.

Eric tossed the menu down on the table just as the door opened. His train of thought stopped when he saw the woman who entered the diner.

Her skin gleamed a rich gold and her dark brown hair fell past her shoulders in thick locks. She was wearing an unbuttoned red-and-black checkered flannel shirt with the sleeves rolled up. Her forearms were corded with muscle. She had on a nondescript gray T-shirt underneath that was tucked into crisp jeans that hugged equally muscular legs. Her hips and chest looked soft and full, though.

Eric shifted in his seat a bit, his mind already primed to be looking for…something. Even from across the room, he could see that her eyes were pale gray, clear and piercing.

Her gaze landed first on the door to the kitchen, then slid across the open space between the dining area and the chefs, where they handed out food to the wait staff. Her glance briefly paused on the entrance to the hall that led to the bathrooms and again on the rear exit.

She was surveying the room, like Eric had just been doing. She wasn't even trying to be subtle about it, though.

Eric leaned back in his chair, resting his hand in his lap for an easier draw—then remembered that he didn't have a weapon.

Shit.

At least he had his handcuffs.

She scanned the crowd, her gaze latching on to his with laser focus. And she smiled.

Eric felt a tightness build in his chest. Not quite dread, but definitely anticipation.

God, she was beautiful.

She started to weave her way toward him, passing waitresses carrying plates filled with eggs and bacon. She stopped suddenly, her eyes going wide as she…sniffed the air. Outright sniffed it, like a hungry animal might.

Beautiful and *strange.*

Eric strained to make out her words through the jumble of noise in the busy diner as she spoke to a waitress.

"What is that?"

The waitress looked irked as she said, "The number seven special."

"Number seven special."

"It's on the menu." When the woman didn't make any sign of moving out of the way, the waitress said, "Do you mind?"

"If I minded your presence, I assure you that you'd know." A near-feral smile twisted the woman's full lips as she watched the waitress back away, then turn and take a different route to her destination.

After a few moments, the woman headed toward Eric again, eyeing the plates of the other customers along the way. She stopped fairly close to him, standing in the empty pathway between the tables, hands at her sides.

It would have been an innocuous pose, except for the way she kept her knees slightly bent and her weight evenly balanced on the balls of her feet—which were encased in black combat boots. From that stance, she could easily spring in any direction she needed.

She held her fingers straight, palms toward him as if she was showing him that she was unarmed. It seemed an almost subconscious gesture, which unnerved him even more.

His gut and his observations told him two things about her right away. She was dangerous and she was not local.

"Eric Peterson," she said.

He waited a few moments before responding, trying to analyze how the situation might play out. He didn't have enough data to form any theories. She obviously knew who he was, so he nodded.

"And you are?"

Her lips twitched up in a mysterious—and somehow taunting—smile.

"Sorca."

"That's it? Just Sorca?"

Instead of elaborating, she lifted her arm and picked at

her sleeve. "This is Brendan's shirt. I wear it as proof of my…friendship with him."

What has Brendan roped me into this time?

"And where is Brendan?" Eric asked.

"Elsewhere. He wanted me to tell you that he's safe."

"Why would he feel the need to let me know that?"

"He said you would worry otherwise. I think he was also afraid you might eventually attack me if you were concerned for his safety." She cast that feral smile at Eric, as if the idea delighted her. And waited.

"I'm not… I'm not going to attack you in the middle of a diner," Eric said.

Her face fell. Was she insane? What kind of game was Brendan playing at, and who the hell had he invited to play?

Sorca shrugged, and said, "I am also to give you this."

She started to reach for the pocket on the front of her shirt. Eric's pulse spiked, his body tingling with adrenaline as he prepared to react, thinking of how to protect the civilians in the diner if she should draw a weapon.

Even though he hadn't moved, she froze, fingers extended again in that, "I come in peace" gesture, despite her seeming eagerness to fight. She kept her arms held out to her sides as she leaned forward.

"Perhaps you would feel better if you retrieved the item yourself. It is in the left pocket of Brendan's shirt."

Eric let out a sigh, a small bit of his tension leaving with it. He still kept himself absolutely ready for an attack as he carefully reached two fingers into her pocket for the piece of paper he could see within it. He did his best to ignore the heat from her body or the closeness of his hand to her breast.

He pulled out the note and flicked it open, keeping her in his line of sight. The message was short and unhelpful.

Eric, this is Sorca. I am safe, but our planet is not. Do as she says and she'll bring you to me.
Brendan
P.S. Brown foxes like boxes more than oxes.

Eric would have dismissed it immediately as one of Brendan's games, except he ended it with one of the codes they had developed for covert communications—an official code meant to let each other know the message was authentic.

Brendan knew he could only use this one once. Why would he waste it on a game?

Talking to Sorca while she was standing next to the table was both awkward and drawing unwanted attention from the nearby patrons. Eric gestured to the empty chair across from him.

"Will you join me?"

One of her dark eyebrows hiked up her forehead. She

stared at a plate sitting on a nearby table and licked her upper lip. Slowly.

The tingling coating Eric's skin turned from pre-fight adrenaline to a blasting heat that coalesced in his groin. If this had been part of a regular assignment—part of a mission—things could get very interesting between them. But this was one of Brendan's games. Probably.

Eric shoved away the physical reaction, not letting himself fully register the thoughts that were behind them— thoughts he couldn't seem to stop, at least as long as he was looking at Sorca. Eating would probably help take his mind off of her .

He slid his menu across the table to her as she sat, and said, "What'll you have?"

Her brow furrowed as she looked at the menu, cocking her head to the side. The smirk vanished from her lips as she studied it—holding it upside-down. Was she pretending that she couldn't read?

With a laugh, she shook her head and tossed the menu back across the table. "Whatever you plan to eat will be fine with me as well."

He flagged down a waitress, and said, "Two number sevens, please."

"Sure thing, handsome." The waitress winked at him before walking away.

"Her eye is spasming," Sorca said. "Is she injured?"

"That was a wink. She's fine."

Sorca's brow furrowed as she stared at him.

"What?" he said.

"You confirmed that you are Eric Peterson."

"I am."

"Then why did that woman call you 'Handsome'?"

"Ouch."

Eric chuckled and Sorca joined in—a few moments late.

Pretending she couldn't read *and* that she didn't understand the word "handsome"? He decided to roll with it.

"It's a descriptive word," he said. "It means she likes how I look."

"How you..." Sorca's brow furrowed again as she glanced around the restaurant before her intense gaze settled back on him. "Your physical appearance. She appreciates your physical appearance."

"That's one way of putting it."

Sorca leaned back in her chair, one eyebrow cocked as she cast her smirk at him. He had never been the subject of a brazen stare before. It was more unsettling than he expected.

He sorted through the rules of the game. Sorca was acting the part of someone unfamiliar with local idioms and customs. There was an odd cadence to her speech—which seemed overly formal—but she didn't have an accent that he could place. In fact, she didn't seem to have any accent at all.

She seemed eager to test herself against him physically. The combat boots and stance warned him not to underestimate her. And the muscles on her arms... He'd never seen such definition on a woman.

Brendan had used one of their codes. Maybe this was some sort of military simulation game? He was heading into dangerous territory by bringing Sorca into it, if she *wasn't* military. She could be someone from an associated project that Eric hadn't met yet...

A strange thrill jolted through him at the thought—half dread, half excitement. He needed more information. And the only way he was going to get it was to play along. He stared across the table at the mysterious woman with the devil-may-care smile.

"You have hair on your face," she said.

He felt his jaw drop open. He snapped it shut, started to speak, then shut his mouth again.

He had training to cover any number of cultural differences. He knew six languages, twenty ways to take down an armed opponent without hurting them, many more ways to do so with...different results. But none of his scenarios, none of his experience, came anywhere close to this woman. The energy she put off was completely alien to him.

"Brendan also has hair on his face," Sorca said. "And another male I know who has been staying in this area for a time. Is this considered handsome?"

Another "male"?

"It depends on your taste," Eric said.

"Hmm. I think I like it." She leaned an elbow on the table, craning her neck to look at the rest of his body. Her gaze heated. "Handsome, indeed."

"Thanks." Under his breath, he added, "I think."

If this was her idea of flirting, it was the strangest, most aggressive conversation he'd ever had.

Flirting... Oh, no.

His stomach sank. Was Brendan trying to set Eric up on a date?

It didn't matter if that's what it was. That was not happening. Even if Sorca was the most gorgeous woman he'd ever seen. Who also gave off an aura of being able to handle herself in a fight. Maybe even combat. She could be *ex*-military...

Her behavior was too bizarre for her to be a foreign operative But there was definitely something not local about her. Like really not local.

She wasn't among the list of Brendan's eccentric friends that Eric had read about during Brendan's background check. Someone new, then. And this was someone Brendan thought would be a good match for Eric?

That theory seemed to be the most plausible. He would have to find a way to let her down easy.

Chapter Two

Such a fascinating Earthling.

Sorca gazed at the *handsome* male sitting across from her. His eyes were brown with a gold tinge, his hair much the same, but his facial hair was darker.

She struggled to call up the words for facial hair. A… bear and mustache. Yes, those were the words. Probably.

Her cultural indoctrination session had been interesting. Vay, the *Arbiter's* cultural programmer, had worked with Sorca for hours, trying to load the proper protocols and translations into her memory. The effort had been tiresome.

How can Vay even call herself a soldier when she's more interested in making friends than waging battle?

There were deeper impulses woven into the very fibers of Sorca's being that would not be overwritten. Her brain was rejecting more and more of the Coalition's subconscious programming, rebelling against the intrusion. Or maybe she'd been cloned so many times that her brainwaves were getting tired of the constant overwriting.

She seemed to lose a little more of herself each time her mind was mapped onto a newly grown body—after her previous one was killed. She wondered if the most recent batch cf genetic engineers would keep trying to make more of her or just finally let her be purged.

The mental blocks to their programming might be tied to the extreme physical strength her Cygnian DNA gave her. She'd never know at this point, and didn't really care to spend additional time learning more about herself.

But this human… She would like to learn more about him.

The waitress had already taken their order, and returned with plates bearing foods unlike anything Sorca had ever seen. Two white nebulas with burning orange-star centers. They were beautiful. Triangles made up of some sort of compressed sand sat next to them, along with strips of a wavy brown substance that gave off the most amazing scent she had ever encountered.

She leaned over her plate and took a deep breath through her nose, breathing out through her mouth to keep the scents in place before taking another long breath. Her eyes rolled shut, the aroma even twining around her tongue, making her salivate.

"I take it you like brunch," Eric said.

She realized she was not behaving the way the Earthlings surrounding her were. In fact, when she glanced at the nearby tables, several humans were laughing, while others stared at her, their eyes as wide as if they'd seen a mated pair of Lyrians propagating.

She snorted at the image, turning her gaze back toward Eric. He didn't seem shocked. Or amused. He just looked... confused.

And handsome.

"Why hands?" Sorca said.

Eric's dark eyebrows rose on his forehead. "Pardon me?"

"What are hands in relation to 'handsome'?"

"I don't know the etymology of it," he said. "You should ask Brendan."

"I will, when I see him next." She gestured at Eric's plate, and said, "Begin."

If he ate first, she could mirror his actions to avoid further unusual behavior on her part.

"I... Uh..." Eric shook his head. "Okay."

He picked up a silver device with several parallel prongs that would make a fairly effective stabbing weapon, and another that looked like a metal stick or some kind of useless knife. The edge was blunt and the hilt had no guard to keep his hand safe should he try to kill something with it.

Eric stabbed one of his white nebulas with the pronged tool, then used the not-quite-functionless knife to cut off a section, which he lifted to his mouth.

"Interesting," she murmured.

"Me eating eggs is interesting?" He let out a short laugh.

The white nebulas were called eggs. She made a mental note, even though she knew it was unlikely she would ever encounter this delightful food again.

He pointed at her plate with his knife, and said, "If you think that's interesting, you should poke one of the yolks with your toast and see what happens."

She looked at her plate, trying to figure out which thing was "toast" and which was "yolk". Perhaps "toast" was the word for the silver pronged item. He'd used his to stab his egg segment and lift it to his mouth. But then, what was "yolk"?

She picked up the silver toast and held it in a killing grasp, quickly striking the triangles on her plate. At the last moment, she remembered to hold back her blow. She didn't want to harm the implements of eating, nor was she ready for Eric to witness her strength.

The metal toast impaled the compressed-sand yolk, a shower of tiny granules breaking off from it as it split in half with a satisfying *crunch*. Sorca looked up at Eric, beaming at her accomplishment.

He still looked confused.

"That's not... Here." He set down his toast and knife, then picked up a piece of his yolk, and said, "Toast."

"Oh."

The compressed-sand triangles were "toast"? Then what was "yolk"? And why would she poke anything with a piece of food?

He pointed at his plate, toward the bright-sun centers of his eggs. "Yolks."

He gently poked the circle of orange with his toast. Thick fluid burst forth, running over the white segments of his eggs.

She sucked in a breath, her gaze darting to her plate. She didn't bother with the toast, but jabbed a finger into the yolk.

It offered little resistance, the somewhat slimy coating giving way beneath her fingernail. The fluid within was hot. More of it gushed out around her finger, flowing over the nebula-white eggs.

She lifted her hand, laughing as the viscous orange goo dripped onto her plate. She darted her finger into her mouth, eager to taste it.

Words failed her, at least in the primitive language they used on this planet. She had no sensory experience to compare with the yolk's smooth texture or the solar storm of its *taste*. Her tongue seemed to come alive for the first time. Prickles of sensation flooded along her arms, the fine hairs standing on end as the follicles beaded.

She pulled her finger from her lips, sucking every last molecule of yolk from its surface. More. She wanted more.

The sound of metal clanging on ceramics brought her attention back to Eric. She opened her eyes to see him leaning back in his chair with both hands over his face. He dropped his palms to the table and shook his head.

"Listen, I don't know what Brendan's up to," he said, "But this... I'm not into this."

She set her hands firmly on the table, mirroring his posture. "What do you think 'this' is?"

He took a long breath and let it out slowly, his gold-brown eyes staring at her intently. "Brendan has been after me to do more R&R. My job doesn't really allow for that."

"Arenar? What is that?"

"Rest and relaxation. R and R."

"Rejuvenation cycles. I see. And you think he has sent me to you to assist with this 'R and R', yes?"

"Didn't he?"

She smirked at him, then picked up a segment of toast and dipped it into the delicious yolk. She thoroughly saturated what she now understood to be the edible carrying mechanism before bringing it to her mouth and slowly taking a bite.

The toast crunched. The sound was immensely satisfying. And the flavor of the yolk was heightened by another smooth substance that had been spread on the toast. There was a saline element to it that countered the thickness of the orange fluid, much like the crisp texture of the toast countered the yolk's smoothness.

She let the bite partially dissolve on her tongue, breathing in deeply through her nose so the aromas of the surroundings could heighten the experience. When the flavors had begun to fade, she finally chewed and swallowed.

Eric stared at her the whole time. He kept his lips shut

tight, but she noted how his pupils dilated.

"Rejuvenation is vital in maintaining optimal performance," she said. "If Brendan believes you need assistance with this, I am happy to cooperate in a variety of ways."

A muscle began to flex along his cheek beneath his bear. Was that the right word? It didn't feel quite so.

Regardless, she wanted to run her fingers along his jaw, to feel its strength. Instead, she ate more of her excellent brunch.

This male was strong—a naturally occurring specimen, generated completely at random who held excellent attributes. Fascinating.

He narrowed his eyes at her. "How exactly do you know Brendan?"

"We are recent acquaintances. One of my colleagues trained with his bondmate."

"Bondmate?"

"Yes." She knew there was a word for it in this region, but couldn't remember it. "Brendan has recently developed a physical and emotional relationship with her."

"That's funny. He never mentioned anyone to me."

Brendan had informed them all that Eric was part of a group that enforced law. It was absurd to her that this fell outside of the military. Why have multiple groups within a society who had overlapping skills when one unit could be trained to fulfill both functions?

Earth could greatly increase the efficiency of their operations if they had access to the genetic engineering techniques of the Sadirians. They could tailor each individual to the task they would be assigned. Although, for a natural specimen, Eric seemed very well suited for the cultural function he had selected. He reminded her of many of the soldiers she served with aboard the *Arbiter*.

She was fairly certain she had raised Eric's suspicions. Her assignment was to bring him to the *Arbiter* so that he could join Earth's newly formed Department of Homeworld Security—or receive a mind-wipe if he refused. Brendan most likely wanted Eric in good condition when he arrived. His cooperation would assist with that.

While she parsed through the scenarios going through her mind, she lifted one of the wavy sticks of...fabric? Eric had eaten a bite of his, so she assumed it was edible.

The smell rising from it sent another thrill through her body. It was even better than the eggs and toast. She took a small bite, the texture requiring her to chew the substance more than the others.

The explosion of flavors shook her. She let out a groan, then shoved more of it into her mouth, chewing rapidly.

"What is this?" She covered her mouth to keep any of its contents from falling out while she spoke around the incredible food substance.

"Bacon."

"Bacon." She practically purred the word, holding

another strip between both hands and snapping it into two pieces.

Her meal was nearly finished, and Eric's suspicions were fully engaged. Daylight would keep her from leaving the planet until nightfall—unless she wanted to break protocol and risk being seen by Earthlings should her ship's cloak fail. Which she didn't.

Originally, she had planned to simply approach Eric, lure him to a secluded spot, and secure him for transport to her ship. She'd imagined it would involve striking him in the head with just enough force to render him unconscious, then carrying him back to her ship.

Now... Now, she had other ideas. She had seen the way General Serath—Adam—and his Earth wife, Evelyn, displayed their bond through touch.

Wife. That was the word she had been looking for when speaking of Brendan's new lifemate.

Sorca had been curious, observing both couples share their affection through light touches and kisses when they thought no one was watching. She had rarely seen them *not* touching, in fact.

She hadn't seen the appeal. But this was just the *food* that Earthlings ate, and the stimulus was beyond anything she'd ever experienced. Outside of combat, anyway.

She had hours to explore more of the environment before she'd be able to fly the skimmer back to the *Arbiter*. She now intended to make good use of them. The opportunity to explore the customs and delights of a planet with preservation status was unlikely to ever come to her again. All that remained was for her to determine how to gain Eric's cooperation.

Chapter Three

Watching Sorca eat was much better than having his own brunch. Eric had never seen someone enjoy their food on such a primal level. The way she was looking at him made him wonder if she was thinking of having him for dessert.

Brendan had strange friends.

Eric still wasn't sure about the point of this whole exercise, though. Was it a blind date? Some sort of weird roleplaying scenario? Both? And where was this woman from that she'd never encountered bacon? There was no way she could have faked that reaction to it.

He'd asked about some of Brendan's pastimes while trying to forge a bond that would keep Brendan working on the project. They'd talked about cosplaying and... Harping? No, larping. Live action role-play.

If that's what this was, Sorca seemed to be going all-out in her role.

Whatever Brendan hoped would come of this, Eric had one objective—get Brendan back to work on the project. Eric could tolerate the weirdness of the whole situation.

And honestly, spending time with Sorca wasn't that bad. Definitely strange, but not unpleasant.

Without looking at her plate, she picked up a piece of egg white, dripping with yolk, and slid it into her mouth. She sucked her finger clean, holding him with that sultry smile for a few moments as she chewed.

"We should copulate." She didn't bother to lower her voice. In fact, she made the proclamation louder than her earlier words had been.

He felt the gazes of several people nearby snap to their table and heard a few gasps. Sorca turned her head in the direction of one of the more scandalized sounds. She leaned toward an older woman sitting at the table next to them.

"You have a strong opinion on the matter," Sorca said. "What is the protocol when you wish to establish a physical relationship with someone?"

Glaring at Sorca, the woman said, "I have no comment."

Her word choice struck Eric as odd—but then, what about today wasn't? She cast a quick glance at him from the corner of her eye. It was probably just the weirdness of the situation, but something about the woman was setting off warning bells in his head. Before he could examine it further, Sorca drew his attention again.

"Eric Peterson." She pushed back from the table, then stood and held out her hand to him. "Come with me."

Letting her down easy wasn't going to be an option. At least if he followed her out, he could avoid making a scene in the diner. He threw a few bills on the table and stood, but didn't take her hand. She didn't seem bothered by that at all. Or by the few cheers or clapping that broke out around them.

He was about to tell the cheering squad to calm down when Sorca lifted her arms in the air and yelled, "Victory!"

He was supposed to keep Brendan safe and focused on his work. After this, Eric might kill Brendan himself.

Eric followed Sorca out of the diner, trying to get his thoughts in order. She walked right into the street, stopping with her hands on her hips and feet spread in a strong stance. A fighter's stance, that seemed again to be second nature.

"Sorca…" His voice trailed off as he realized a truck was bearing down on her. She was standing in the middle of the street. "Sorca!"

He sprinted for her just as she noticed the vehicle. She turned toward him and leapt from the street, hitting him in the ribs and knocking the wind from him. He swore he was off his feet for several seconds as she carried him back toward the building, fast.

The next thing he knew, the brick wall of the restaurant was abrading his skin through his thin shirt—and Sorca was pressed against his chest, one arm wrapped tightly around his waist. She was muscular, but tiny. He hadn't realized how short she was until they stood side-by-side. Well, face-to-chest.

He was panting from the adrenaline, a dull ache in his ribs where she'd impacted. She merely looked up at him and smiled.

"That's an interesting transport," she said. "Its mass and velocity make it dangerous. You must not risk yourself for me. You aren't replaceable."

"And you are?"

She laughed, as if the brush with the truck had been nothing "You would be surprised."

What did it take to rattle her? When the people in the diner were judging her, when the waitress tried to intimidate her, even the cheerleaders for her victory shout, she didn't seem to care at all. Eric couldn't imagine what it must be like to live like that.

"It'll catch up with you eventually," he said.

"What will?"

"Living like you've got nothing to lose."

"Perhaps. But what a race it will be to the end." She laughed, bringing her free hand to his face to run a finger along his jaw. "Now, come with me. I have things to discuss with you that are not for others' ears."

What the hell? It was all part of the game, and he really did feel that he needed to find out what was going on. At least she'd stopped talking about "copulating". Not that the idea was off-putting *per se*...

"Fine," he said. "Take me to Brendan."

She stepped up on her toes, sniffing Eric's chest as she

did. Her nose grazed his collarbone, setting off a chain reaction of goosebumps. Her arm was still wrapped around his waist, her body pressed against his.

She let out another of those self-satisfied purrs, but this time it was all about *him*. The attention was unsettling in the best and worst ways at once.

She might not be talking about copulating anymore, but he was pretty sure she was still thinking about it. Unfortunately, so was he.

"Eventually," she said. "I wish to experience more of the pleasures your homew— Your home has to offer."

For the first time, she'd stumbled over something, actually stopped herself instead of acting on whatever whim seemed to catch her fancy. She glanced around, as if checking to make sure no one had overheard her.

"Home-" something. What had she been about to say?

She stepped away from him, but grasped his wrist and pulled him after her. "There is a park nearby. It will give us privacy for our conversation and...rejuvenation."

"Rejuvenation?"

Her gaze slowly passed down his body before returning to his eyes. "Arenar is important to maintain peak efficiency."

He let her pull him away from the wall. "Why do I have a feeling I'm going to regret this?"

"Your feeling is inaccurate. I promise you pleasure. There will be no regrets."

He let out a laugh as he fell in step beside her. He couldn't help himself.

"Are you always this confident?" he said.

"It is well earned."

After they had walked for several minutes, she turned from the sidewalk onto a walking path that led into a forest. A wave of misgiving passed through him. No one was nearby, and the trail probably wasn't heavily used this time of day. It would be a great place for an ambush.

When he hesitated, she said, "You have nothing to fear from me. I am sworn to protect you."

That was a change from what he was used to. He was always the one cast in the role of protector.

He snorted, remembering that it was all part of the game. He started walking again, certain Brendan was somewhere in the woods, waiting for them to arrive. Eric just hoped there were no costumes involved. That would be awkward.

"Sworn to Brendan?" Eric asked.

She laughed. "Of course not. Sworn to my commanding officer, General Serath."

"When did Brendan get the promotion?"

"I don't understand."

"I was making a joke. I assume Brendan will be playing the role of General Serath?"

"Playing the role?" Her eyebrows hitched up her forehead and her mouth dropped open. She started to laugh.

And kept going, until she'd doubled over.

"Brendan could never pass for..." She struggled to catch her breath. "I mean..."

"Now *I* don't understand," Eric said. He felt like he should be irked, but her laughter was so pure, he felt himself smiling instead.

She shook her head as she straightened. "You will when you see Serath."

"I look forward to it."

"I suppose I should be calling him 'Adam', since that is the name he has now chosen for himself. I don't know that I will ever think of him as anything other than Serath."

"Have you worked with him for long?"

"I have."

There was warmth in her tone when she spoke of this "Serath". Maybe she did care about something. Odd that Eric felt a bit of a twinge at the thought of her caring for another man when they had *just* met and he was still fairly convinced that she was crazy.

The trail branched off, one path a gentle slope, and the other heading up at a steep angle. Sorca headed for the steep path. She was leading him deeper into the forest. The hike quickly went from pleasant to annoying as sweat trickled between his shoulder blades. She still didn't seem winded at all.

"No one's around," he said. "Why don't you tell me more about what's going on here?" He needed to know the rules of the game if he was going to play.

"You know Brendan has been trying to contact an advanced alien species."

Oh, here we go...

Aliens. He should have guessed it when Brendan's note mentioned the planet being in danger. When she'd stopped herself earlier, he would bet she'd been about to say, "Homeworld".

"Everybody needs a hobby," Eric said. "What of it?"

"He succeeded."

"Of course he did."

"You're not surprised?" She glanced over at him, a puzzled look on her face.

"He's a genius, especially with communications systems. If anyone could make contact with aliens, it would be Brendan."

"Your faith in him is encouraging. But a knowledge of technology will not be sufficient for him to lead Earth's First Contact Committee."

"First contact? Oh, right. With the aliens." Eric managed to keep himself from snorting.

Brendan and his...friend...had obviously put a lot of thought and effort into this. Sorca was absolutely throwing herself into the part. She sounded and acted like she believed every word she said. Every crazy word.

"So, are you one of those aliens he contacted?" Eric asked.

"I am."

"Convenient that you happen to look like an Earthling."

"It is." She nodded, taking the comment totally seriously. "Being able to move about freely with most Earthlings none the wiser will assist us in protecting your planet."

"From what?"

Even though it was a game, Eric still felt a tremor of misgiving flow through him. He lived every day with more knowledge of the precarious balance of human existence on Earth than most people had to deal with. The thought of aliens joining the mix—with their own ways, needs, and agendas—was unnerving.

"Brendan and Serath will provide you with the details," she said. "But first..."

She stepped off the trail into a small clearing. The grass had actually been mowed. It grew thick where the trees didn't block the sun overhead.

"Nice park," he said.

She smiled at him over her shoulder, walking deeper into the field. "Kira told me about this. 'Blades of grass'. I wish to experience it."

"Experience it how?"

Sorca sat and untied her boots, then pulled them off and tossed them aside. Her socks quickly followed. Digging her toes into the greenery surrounding her, she let out a long sigh. The acerbic remark he'd been about to make stuck on his tongue when she smiled up at him. It was such a genuine look of happiness.

Damn, she was a good actress.

"Join me," she said. "The blades are cool and do not cut."

"I'm aware. This is my planet, remember?"

She laughed as she stood. "What is an everyday occurrence for you is something I have never experienced." She looked down at her feet, lifting one then the other slowly, almost as if she was kneading the ground. "It tickles!"

For a fraction of a second, he wondered if this really was a game. Her joy seemed so authentic. He couldn't read any signs of deceit in her expressions—and he'd been trained to detect them.

But that would mean she *was* an alien. That would be crazy.

"Join me." She reached her hand to him.

This was all part of the game. Brendan was going all-out to help Eric relax and have some fun. He might as well enjoy himself.

"What the hell." He pulled off his shoes and threw them on the pile she had created.

"And the fiber covering," she said.

"Fiber covering? Oh, you mean my socks."

"Socks. Yes."

"You really are thinking of everything."

"It's a simple matter. You will enjoy the grass more if it comes in direct contact with your skin. And I did promise you pleasure."

Heat coursed through him again. There were all kinds of pleasure he could think of that he would love to enjoy with a strong, beautiful woman. Even if she seemed a little...off.

Because she was an alien.

Right.

He pulled off his socks and tossed them on the pile. The grass was cool beneath his feet, blades prickling along the sides. It did feel good, and some of his tension eased.

Sorca let Brendan's shirt slide to the ground. Maybe she wanted to feel the wind better or—

Eric's thoughts froze as she pulled her own shirt over her head and dropped it on the growing pile of clothing. The sun seemed to caress the smooth skin of her back, highlighting the lines of her muscles and shoulder blades. She turned, her arms stretched toward the sun, giving him a glorious view of her full breasts.

"Stars, this feels amazing," she said.

Eric stammered for a moment, only finding words when she started to unfasten her jeans. "Sorca, what are you doing?"

"Removing my clothing. You should do the same."

"Wait, what?"

He had thought she was kidding with her talk of copulating and pleasure. But then, she certainly did look extremely happy—even with something as simple as feeling the grass on her feet and the sun on her skin.

She pushed down her jeans and stepped out of them. Instead of standing again, she dropped to the ground and stretched.

"What the hell are you doing?"

"Enjoying the grass." She propped herself up on one elbow. "What are you doing?"

Honestly? He was enjoying watching her enjoying the grass.

The sun gleamed along the line of her side and hips. He wanted to trace it with his fingers, to feel the mix of strength and softness he could see with his eyes. He wanted to roll her over in the soft grass and…copulate.

Chapter Four

Earth was even better than Sorca imagined. She hoped she would make it back to one of the recording pods in a reprogramming center before she inevitably met up with something that killed her. She wanted to keep these memories in the next body the Coalition grew for her.

And she wanted to make more memories. With Eric.

She stood and slowly approached him.

He let out a nervous laugh and shook his head. "Look, if this is all part of the game—"

"Everything is." The words came out sharper than she'd intended, emotions that she needed to suppress roiling beneath the surface.

She had lost count of how many versions of herself she'd been. With the way her mind was rejecting even the simplest of cultural programming sessions like the one that prepared her for Earth, she had a feeling there wouldn't be many more.

His smile faded as she drew near. When she was close enough to feel his body heat, she stopped.

"You are unlike most of the sentients I have

encountered," she said.

"So, you want to have sex with me because I'm an exotic Earthling."

His tone did not sound eager or excited. He seemed… annoyed. Perhaps if she flattered him…

"You are strong and hairy," she said. "I like your bear."

"I truly have no idea how to respond to that."

"Your bear and mustache."

"*Beard* and mustache," he said.

"Beard and mustache," she repeated. She struggled to find the right words, then remembered what the waitress had said at the diner. "Handsome. You are handsome."

He snorted and one eyebrow arched up his forehead. "Thanks, I guess."

"Do you not find me handsome as well?"

He outright laughed, his smile crinkling the corners of his eyes. "That isn't the word I would use."

Her chest felt tight, her heart suddenly beating faster against her ribs.

How could she be able to feel disappointment about this still? The muscles obviously visible beneath her skin made her a freakish specimen among her kind. Those who were intrigued by her physicality saw her only as a curiosity— especially when they learned of her Cygnian DNA.

Eric had seemed so different from those people. She had hoped he would be different in this regard as well.

She did her best to discard the useless emotions. The…

longing.

She wanted to beat on something—to smash it beyond recognition.

"I see," she said. "Among my people, my musculature is also considered unattractive."

She started to step away, but he grabbed her arm. His grip was firm at first, but gentled when she looked up at him.

"You're the most beautiful woman I've ever seen."

"*Beautiful.* I know this word." It was a high compliment among his kind. "Are you certain you're using it correctly?"

He laughed. "Yes, I'm sure."

He brushed her hair past her shoulder, letting his thumb trail along her cheek. The touch was shockingly gentle. She grabbed his wrist and pulled his hand away.

"I'm sorry," he said. "I thought you wouldn't mind, since you said you wanted to…"

"Copulate." She remembered the phrase he had used. "Have sex. Yes."

"Touching is generally involved in that."

"Of course."

Perhaps with Earth-sex.

The Coalition provided everyone with a drug they called *Coupling* to handle their biological urges. Most citizens used it alone, but some preferred enjoying the experience with a partner. Since the drug handled all stages of arousal, including culmination, there wasn't much interaction required.

Sorca had always found using *Coupling* unsatisfactory, even with a partner. Her body chemistry seemed to resist its effects. She had an even worse reaction to *Balance*—the drug used to maintain emotional equilibrium among the populace.

She released Eric's wrist, wondering if he would touch her like that again, his fingers as light as breath against her skin.

"I'm not saying we're going to have sex."

She smirked at him. "Your pupils are extremely dilated and your breath rate has increased."

"Sorca..."

"What is your preferred protocol?"

"My 'preferred protocol' doesn't usually involve a woman being absolutely committed to playing her role as an alien looking for an Earth hook-up."

"Hook-up?"

"Sex, Sorca." He shook his head. "This is really weird."

"Are you interested in copul—in having sex with me or are you not?"

He let out a sigh, and said, "Yes."

A thrill of victory sparked along her nerves. She leaned in closer, till the fabric of his shirt whispered across her flesh.

"Whether you believe I'm an alien who is profoundly

interested in sharing this pleasure with you or that I'm a woman playing a role, it would seem you have only one decision to make."

"Which is?"

"Whether you want to play along."

He laughed briefly, but then lifted his free hand to her shoulder. He still held her arm in a gentle grip.

"You really want this?" he said.

"The pleasures of Earth. I wish to experience them with you. To share them."

He shook his head. "What the hell."

He leaned in and pressed his lips against hers. A kiss, like Sorca had seen Serath and Evelyn exchange.

Eric's lips were a bit dry, but soft. He moved them against hers like his thumb had caressed her cheek. He ran his hands down her arms, then around to her back, pulling her close.

The embrace locked them together. She didn't like the idea that she would have to use her strength to break his hold. To even the battlefield, she wrapped her arms around his neck, drawing him closer. Now they both held the other captive.

Perhaps her action had a hidden meaning, because he let out a small groan and slid his tongue across her lips. She gasped at the strangeness of the feeling, and he thrust his tongue into her mouth.

She would have thought it would be appalling to have

someone else's tongue in her mouth, but instead warmth spread through her. One of his hands slid down to her buttocks, gripping her firmly and pushing her against his erection.

They were having sex with their mouths. She hadn't known such a thing was possible. But the movements of his tongue, her body's response to his presence within her...

She ran her fingers through his hair, grabbing a handful of the dark strands and tilting his head to the side— carefully. The last thing she wanted was to injure him. He groaned again, but instead of deepening the kiss, he shifted his face so that his lips were pressed against her neck.

More warmth. More tingling sensations as the follicles of her skin drew to attention.

Slickness was gathering between her legs. As if he sensed it, he...moved his hand there. She gasped as he pressed his fingers within the folds of her flesh, parting them, delving deeper until—

"Stars!"

He was within her again, in a way she had never imagined. Spreading her, moving inside and out. His fingers pumped like a piston while his thumb circled a nerve cluster she hadn't known she possessed. All the bodies she had gone through, all the lifetimes, and she had never experienced this part of herself.

At some point, she had released his hair, and was now half-wrapped around him. She wasn't sure when it had happened. She only knew she must be careful with him.

She wrapped her arms around his shoulders—positioning her body so that she wouldn't hurt him too badly if she forgot herself again. Something was building within her, and she had already lost awareness of herself once.

His pace increased, his fingers flexing deep in her core, stretching her, spreading her slickness. The energy he was building intensified. Warmth and tingling, sparks and plasma bursts, until it coalesced in a white-hot explosion that fired out from his hand at her center, through her entire body.

She screamed, barely registering the answering calls of startled birds that leapt from the trees into the air. He grunted, lowering her to the ground and kneeling between her parted legs.

"I didn't hurt you, did I?" he said.

She was confused at first, hearing the words running through her own mind spoken by him. Why would he think he had hurt her?

The physical sensations he had generated within her were joined by something deeper, stronger. An emotional resonance she hadn't anticipated.

He cared. He cared if he hurt her.

"You didn't cause me pain," she said. "You gave me pleasure unlike anything I've ever experienced."

He was panting, his hands fisted on his thighs as he

gazed at her. His eyes held hunger.

"I promised you pleasure," she said. "That I would share this with you."

Eric nodded as he rose on his knees. He unfastened his jeans and shoved them down his thighs. His member jutted at her, the tip glistening.

She had never seen this part of a male so close. When she had used *Coupling*, she had barely had time to bring her partner into her body before the drug completed their mating activities for them.

Eric was glorious.

He reached into his back pocket and pulled out the small folded bit of fabric where he kept his currency. He opened it and pulled out a small square of metal. No, not metal, from the way he tore it open. Something she hadn't encountered.

He pulled a small circle of pliable material from the shiny square. After pressing the circle to the tip of his erection, he rolled it down, covering himself.

When they were finished, she'd have to ask what it was. For now, she was more interested in action than knowledge.

"Are you sure you want to do this?" he said.

She laughed. "How can you even ask?"

"I always ask."

"Then here is your answer, Eric Peterson. Yes."

He dropped his body onto hers, pressing against her core. She could feel the strain thrumming through his body, mirrored in her own. Red clouded her vision as he entered her—for once, not battle rage. Something else. Something new.

It was like flickering plasma running over her skin—energy that didn't burn or hurt, but made her feel alive in a way she'd never felt before. She wanted more of it, wanted to grab him and pull him closer, deeper. And she was afraid if she did, she'd snap him right in two.

As he pressed himself into her, he groaned. "God, you're so tight. My cock's going to go off any second."

"Your what?"

"My dick. You just…feel too good." His eyes were pinched shut and he held himself completely still, as if he was struggling with his own self-control.

She tried to piece together his meaning. "You're about to orgasm."

Her body was pulsing, preparing for its own release.

He let out a laugh and shook his head. "Yes, if you want to be specific about it. Thanks for the distraction. It's helping."

"I will assist you in prolonging this experience."

For once, she had no idea what action to take. Among the Sadirians, she was considered to be bizarrely attuned to her body. Her physicality was what made her of greatest use to the Coalition, after all. In battle, she always knew what to do. But this was an entirely different physical experience.

Eric was taking slow breaths, still not moving. She could feel a deep throb from his dick resonating within her.

Finally, she admitted her ignorance. "I don't know what to do."

He opened his eyes as he let out a snort. "Be less beautiful? Less soft and strong at once. Less confident and sexy and...oddly vulnerable."

"I can't change those things—"

"I was kidding. I wouldn't change anything about you."

"Nothing?"

"No. Not even your bizarre personality."

"There must be something you would improve upon."

While they were working on Sorca's hybridized DNA, the genetic engineers in the Coalition had tried repeatedly to improve upon her abilities and form, often with... unfortunate results.

Several times, they had implanted her memories and persona in those forms. Sometimes, she would survive long enough to be sent to a recording center and update her mental imprint. She suppressed a shiver, pushing the thoughts away.

She didn't want this memory to be tainted by the past. Eric started speaking again, drawing her attention back to the moment.

"I want to say I'd make your pussy have less firm of a grip, but that would be a lie. I've never felt anything so good."

Slowly, he pulled his hips back. The movement was distressing at first, until the friction struck her nerves, making her gasp. She grabbed at his back, instinctively trying to keep him close. At the last moment, she remembered to only take hold of his shirt.

He sank back into her with a rocking motion. She gasped at the waves of stimulation pulsing through her body, the odd heaviness in her limbs and fullness in her chest.

"Stars…" she said.

"Damn…"

"This can not end."

He kissed her neck and held his lips close to her ear. "We can always do it again."

"Can we?"

"As many times as you want."

"I wish to do this *many* times."

"I better pick up more condoms, then."

"Condoms?"

"You don't have to keep pretending to be an alien. This activity is absolutely entertaining enough for me."

"I never said I was pretending."

He laughed and shook his head.

Again, he lifted his hips, pulling his dick from her. And again, he slid back in, as deep as was possible. She felt him filling her, pushing against the muscles of her core as they gripped him.

He repeated the motion a few times, increasing his speed. The pulses moving along her nerves intensified, pleasure beating against her senses. He lifted himself on one elbow while he reached with his other hand to grip her thigh and pull her leg up along his side.

"Wrap your leg around me," he said.

"I can't."

"Sure you can. You don't have to be that flexible."

"It isn't that. I don't want to hurt you."

He laughed, pausing in his movements. He took a few deep breaths, perhaps trying to calm his body.

Sorce didn't want to calm her body. She wanted to experience what was just on the other side of the waves of energy rippling through her from where they were joined.

"You don't have to worry about hurting me," he said.

"I always have to worry about hurting those near me," she said. "Especially during this."

His brow furrowed as he thought on her words. He had yet to see her strength.

"I'm not like you," she said.

"Because you're an alien?"

She nodded. The plasma waves were ebbing, and for a brief moment, she wondered if she did want them back. Perhaps it would be better to just walk away now, before she completed their coupling—*sex*—knowing she would never experience anything like it again.

He tightened his grip on her thigh, holding it tight

against his side, then pressed his chest against hers, crushing his hips to hers. The nerve cluster reawakened with a cascade of plasma bursts throughout her body.

No, she should definitely complete this encounter.

Eric grabbed the back of her neck, bringing them as close together as was safely possible, then he rolled over, pulling her along with him while they were joined. He let out a grunt as she instinctively adjusted her weight, straddling him.

Her muscles were denser than a standard Earthling or Sadirian. It increased her effectiveness in battle, but made her heavier than someone her size would normally be. She wouldn't crush him, but didn't want to make him uncomfortable.

She raised herself on her elbows as he released her thigh, bringing his hands to her hips. He was smiling at her.

"I don't understand why you performed that maneuver," she said.

"You seemed worried about my safety. Worry isn't very good when it comes to enjoying yourself. I figured if you take over, you'll feel better."

"How do I—"

She leaned back and the motion pushed him even deeper into her core. Her spread legs opened her slit so that the nerve cluster he had so expertly stimulated earlier was pressed against his pelvis. More bursts of plasma. Heat pulsed along her skin with each touch and gyration.

"Cygnus X..."

"I'm guessing that means you like it?" Eric smirked up at her.

"Yes," she groaned.

"And this?" He pressed his thumb into her slit, rubbing the nerve cluster. Her body thrummed like a phase rifle powering up to full.

"Eric..." Her eyes drifted shut, all her senses pulling inward, to where they were joined.

"Move on me, Sorca. It's okay. I promise."

She kept her hands at her sides, gazing down along her body to where she could see him buried deep inside, and smiled.

"Earthling, you have no idea what you're in for."

Chapter Five

Eric had maybe five seconds to ponder that "I-know-something-you-don't-know" smile of hers. Five seconds of holding his breath before she took his advice and started to move.

She rose up on her thighs, the movement pulling along his dick in a stroke that nearly ended him. Then she cautiously lowered herself back down, her body pressing against his shaft, all softness and strength and heat.

If he hadn't been wearing a condom, he wouldn't have lasted ten seconds with her. As humiliating as that experience might be, he was more tempted to try it with her than with anyone else he'd ever had sex with.

Her dark hair fell across her chest as she became more confident in her strokes. He brought his hands to her breasts, lifting them and kneading them. When he gently pinched her nipples between his fingers, she gasped and increased her pace.

How could anything feel so good? Gooseflesh spread over his arms as the energy building in him crested.

She threw her head back and let out a primal scream, her

core pulsing, coaxing him to his own climax. It hit him like a sonic boom, vibrating in every molecule of his body. She kept pulling on him, pumping him, her body not giving him any escape from the pleasure cascading along every nerve ending.

It was hard to breathe. His vision dimmed around the edges as his orgasm went on and on.

Finally, she slowed, then stopped, barely panting.

"Are you all right?" she said.

"I'm not sure."

Physically he felt...amazing. Almost like their bodies had fused where they connected. The afterimage of the pleasure they had shared was so intense he didn't even mind the thought. Which *did* bother him.

He couldn't afford to get that wrapped up in anyone. He had a job to do, people to protect.

Sorca lifted her hips. Normally, he would have slid from his partner at that point, but with her, it was just a continuation of what had come before. He felt every millimeter as their bodies...disengaged, for lack of a better word.

Damn, he'd really been sucked into the whole alien thing.

She rose and took a few steps away, stretching her arms to the sky again. He sat up, gauging how weak his legs would feel when he stood. Her core was right at eye level. Even after that amazing sex—or maybe because of it—all he could think about for that moment was grabbing her by her ass and pulling her to his mouth.

"You have an angry look to you, Eric. Was our sex not satisfactory?"

He was angry, but with himself. He'd never let himself get so carried away with something like this before. He wasn't even sure what "this" was.

"Satisfactory isn't the word I would choose."

She actually looked a bit concerned, her face bearing no trace of her sultry smile and the slightest crease appearing between her eyebrows.

"Did I err?"

"What? No, you didn't do anything wrong. You did everything right, in fact."

Very, very right.

"Then why do you look upset?"

"Because that was spectacular. And you have ruined me for Earth women forever."

Slowly, she smiled. Eric felt it like a blow to the chest. The edge of mischief was missing. Instead of looking amused, she looked *happy*. Fulfilled. And he had helped her to achieve that—in the most pleasurable of ways.

He was in trouble.

"I want to learn more," she said. "When can we have sex again?"

Deep trouble.

"Sorca, I—"

She held her hand to him, as if to help him up. He figured he'd humor her, and took it.

The next thing he knew, he was on his feet. He might have even been *off* his feet for a moment, just like when she'd leapt out of the way of that bus earlier. How strong was she? She didn't seem to notice his confusion, and kept right on with the conversation.

"You enjoyed it, correct?" she said.

"Well, yes."

"Then why should we not couple—I mean have sex—again?"

Couple? More odd phrasing. And she said it so naturally.

Eric had been trained to notice when people were lying. He'd assumed that she was so into her part that she wasn't giving any tells. But now, he could see what it was like when she was experiencing a genuine emotion. He'd seen it in that smile.

She hadn't broken character at all. So that meant... what? That she really was an alien?

He laughed at himself internally as he tried to think of anything but sinking into her heat again.

"For one thing, I only had the one condom," he said.

"Condom. You mentioned this before."

He pulled out his handkerchief, then peeled the condom off of his dick. He briefly flicked his wrist in a, "this" gesture. There weren't any trashcans around, so he wrapped it up and put it in one of his front pockets.

"What is its function?" Sorca's excitement hadn't diminished. And she *still* hadn't broken character.

The more emotion she showed, the more holes he should be seeing in her game. But instead, she seemed more sincere. A weird feeling of misgiving started to grow in him as he fastened his jeans.

"Can we quit with the games?" he said. "I mean, after..."coupling", I'd kind of like to know the real you."

A bit of mischief sparked in her smile again. "I will answer your questions if you answer mine."

"Fine. Within reason. But first, you have to get dressed."

"All right."

She gathered up her clothes and dressed with surprising speed and almost military efficiency. Eric shook off the thought, his misgiving growing.

When she was dressed, she turned to him and said, "What is a condom for?"

"Oh, for crying out..." He shook his head. "It prevents pregnancy and the spread of disease."

"Aha! Then we don't need them for sex. I am free from any Earth-borne pathogens, and will be purged of anything I'm exposed to from our encounters after my first sleep cycle in a regen bed when I return to my ship." She grinned at him, fists on her hips in a victorious stance.

"Sorca, come on." He let out a sigh.

If Brendan had expected them to become a couple, he'd picked a very strange woman for this bizarre blind date—

and that was what it felt like to Eric at this point. Sure, on the one hand, things were going great physically, but emotionally and mentally, how was he supposed to connect...

"Wait, what about pregnancy?" he said. "Why doesn't that worry you?"

"The genetic engineers sterilized me during my design. There are specific laws which govern the DNA they used in my creation. They can't risk it being spread, stolen, or manipulated outside of their labs. My body even has a self-destruct and will disintegrate me should either my heartbeat or brainwaves end."

Cold chills rocketed down his spine at the thought. He actually shivered, until he reminded himself that this was all just a game.

Eric had a natural instinct to protect people. And even though this was all a messed up fantasy scenario, he still felt something in him reaching toward her, wanting to protect her.

"I don't know what's more disturbing," he said. "That your fantasy involves such a fucked up system or that you're pretending you don't have a problem with it."

He really was in it too deep. But not so deep that he was okay making light of such a serious topic. Apparently, she took it pretty seriously too, because when her smile faded, it was replaced by a menacing glare.

"I am a soldier for the Coalition of Planets," Sorca said.

"Chief of Security for the fleet's flagship, the *Arbiter*, under command of General Serath, who has enforced peace in this galaxy more effectively than any officer in Coalition history."

"I get it. So you serve the very monsters who created you."

"I was *created* to serve."

The world she was describing was horrible. He shook his head, as if that could clear it of the civilization she'd described.

"I don't understand why this distresses you," she said. "Everyone in the Coalition has all they need. Every citizen has purpose."

"Purpose is not the same as meaning. Why am I even playing along with this?" He took a few steps away before turning back to her. "Truth, Sorca. I wanted *truth* when I asked my questions, not more games."

"I have only spoken truth to you, Eric Peterson. And to say otherwise insults my honor."

"That's enough. I'm out. Tell Brendan I'll contact him tomorrow about—"

As he walked past her, she grabbed his arm, freezing his chain of thought. Freezing it because she was holding him in place—*with one hand.*

Cautiously, he pulled against her grip, just to test out how bad of a mess he'd gotten himself into. She didn't budge. Instead, her grip tightened enough to send arcs of pain up his arm.

"Brendan has requested your presence on the *Arbiter*." Her voice was low and her lips curled up in a near snarl. "I am under orders from General Serath to bring you to the ship. Know that I speak the truth when I say, I *will* bring you to the ship. I do not fail in my missions."

His stomach felt leaden. Was she insane? And if she was, had she done something to Brendan?

Eric knew several ways to break her hold on him—ways that would counteract her strength. But it might be better to play along. Maybe he could get her to take him to Brendan, since that's what she seemed to be so focused on.

Her expression softened as she seemed to shake herself. She looked at her hand on his arm and loosened her grip so that it wasn't quite as painful. When she spoke, her voice was gentler as well.

"I'm sorry. I don't want to hurt you. The amount of reprogramming I've had is having unforeseen effects on my capacity for emotional control."

"Reprogramming? So, what, are you an android now?"

"Of course not. Androids are much too expensive to create and maintain."

"So, the Coalition just creates *people* to serve it. Disposable people."

Her only response was a tightening of her lips.

"I'm torn right now, Sorca. Because I really don't want you to be crazy. But if you're telling the truth…"

That thought was so much more frightening.

She stepped close to him, running the fingers of her free hand along his cheek. "I will protect you, Eric. As much as I'm able. But I have to follow orders."

"And if you're ordered to kill me?"

"It won't come to that. At worst, you'll receive a mind-wipe and forget all that's passed between us. But I'll remember. Even through death."

Yeah. She was crazy.

Before he had a chance to say more, she ducked down and hefted him in a fireman's carry, draping him across her shoulders. He was so surprised by her speed and strength that he didn't even have a chance to react.

How the hell was she carrying him? *Effortlessly.* She headed back to the trail, without a single hitch in her stride.

"Sorca, put me down."

"I'm sorry it has to be this way. I think it will be safest for you if I carry you to my ship. Once you see it, you'll know I'm telling the truth. And there's so much more you need to know."

"Such as?" He looked around for anything he could use to help himself get free. She had that grip of steel on one of his arms, but he could strike at her with the other.

"Earth is being invaded by hostile aliens," she said.

"Like ones that abduct you after the most amazing sex of your life?"

He couldn't believe he'd already had sex with her. But

he hadn't known that she was… Crazy? An alien? Neither option was appealing.

"I'm pleased you enjoyed yourself so much. It was also my most pleasurable experience. Even better than bacon."

He snorted despite his situation.

Aliens. Right.

He saw a flash of gray fur in the brush next to them and his heart picked up in response. Craning his neck for a better look, he saw that it was just a deer. A weirdly pale, not-bothered-by-humans deer, but still just a deer.

He was definitely letting this all get to him. How the hell was she still carrying him, though?

"I'm not your enemy," she said. "The *Arbiter* is here to assist. General Serath fell in love with an Earthling during his shore leave here. Earth is now special to him and he will do everything in his power to protect it."

"Great."

"Brendan needs your help to sort out how to handle the situation."

"And how did Brendan get involved?"

"He made contact with the soldier who was operating our listening station."

"That makes as much sense as anything else, I guess."

He needed to keep her talking while he figured out a plan for what to do next. If she'd done something to Brendan, Eric couldn't kill her. Not until he found and retrieved his asset.

The thought tugged on his heart with surprising strength, like the woman carrying him. He didn't want to have to kill Sorca. And he wanted Brendan to be okay—not just as an asset, but as a friend.

"And I'm sure Brendan won him over with his charming personality," Eric said.

"*Her*. Kira is the woman Brendan has pair-bonded with. They fell in love while conversing using his encoded communications array."

Fuck.

How the hell did Sorca know about that? *She should not know about that.*

Eric wasn't the only one in deep water. Brendan was way out there, too—surrounded by sharks. If he'd shared information about the classified projects he was working on... There was nothing Eric could do to protect Brendan.

Eric revisited the possibility that Sorca was an enemy agent. And immediately dismissed it. The entire situation was too bizarre.

Sorca kept on talking, not winded by carrying Eric's weight while walking uphill. His feet were almost dragging on the ground.

"Apparently, Earthlings have quite an effect on Sadirians," she said. "Since Earthlings are initially of the same species, I suppose it makes a bit of sense."

"The same species?"

"A colony ship crashed on your planet millennia ago.

The Sadirians who survived lost touch with their origins as they assimilated with the environment and took over from the evolving hominids."

"Of course they did."

The ground bounced along below, the trail left behind as she ventured into the brush. She managed to avoid most of the low-hanging branches that might have hit him, and the foliage seemed to be thinning.

She wasn't bothering with trying to restrain him as she carried him. Either she didn't know any better or—the more alarming possibility—she didn't see him as any kind of threat. He kept running through various scenarios of ways he could get free, with different levels of physical ramifications for her.

"You're like a glimpse into the past," she said. "Back when Sadirians actually interacted on a more intimate physical and emotional level. I must say, having now experienced this myself, I understand the appeal. I was curious about whether something similar would occur between us when I received the assignment."

"Wait, you mean falling in love? Because sex in a park isn't the same as falling in love." Even super hot sex.

"Don't be ridiculous. My duty is to my ship and to General Serath."

"And the Coalition."

She shrugged, accidentally digging her shoulder into his stomach. He let out a grunt and she stopped.

"Did I hurt you?" she said.

"Yes."

She set him down, negating his need for any of the plans he'd been working on to escape her clutches. Well, to a point. She still had a grip on one of his wrists. He looked around at where they'd stopped, trying to get his bearings.

The trail was long gone. They had emerged from the trees at the top of a cliff. There was only a narrow space a few yards wide with sparse grass between the forest and a sheer drop-off.

What the hell did she plan to do next?

Chapter Six

"Nice view," Eric said. "Do you mind if I get a better look?"

"Proceed." Sorca didn't see the harm in Eric exploring his surroundings. She would be curious as well, if their roles were reversed.

She let go of his wrist, but walked at his side, just in case he should try to run. He didn't seem like the running kind, however. A thrill shot through her as she wondered if he was the type who might issue a challenge to her instead. She'd felt his body tense a few times while carrying him, as if he was considering an attempt at breaking away from her hold.

They stopped near the cliff's edge and looked out at the hillside. Sharp rocks dotted the ground at least a dozen meters below them. It would be best not to fall.

The skimmer was close. She'd flown it in over the cliff, landing in a large clearing they could easily reach by walking along the space between the trees and the drop-off. When it was time to leave, she'd have a clear path. And the ship was also far enough out of the way that it was unlikely

Earthlings would accidentally discover it.

"Protocol dictates that we leave at nightfall," she said. "That way, if the ship's cloak fails, Earthlings are less likely to notice the skimmer."

"Let me guess. Your ship is right next to us, but it's cloaked."

"No, it's meters away, in a larger cleared area. If it were that close, the cloak would have disengaged after sensing my proximity."

He laughed and shook his head. The light caught in his hair. She hadn't truly tested it to see if it was as soft as it looked. She hoped she would still have a chance.

Something in the way he was standing made her tense. There was a quiet readiness to him, an ease that belied impending action.

"I caution you against trying to attack me," she said, even though the thought of it sent another wave of excitement through her.

Their physical interactions had already been intense beyond anything she'd experienced. The idea of having the opportunity to face him in combat was...stimulating.

"If I try to leave, will you try to stop me?" he said.

"I will not try. I will succeed."

He snorted and shook his head. "Damn, you're cocky."

In case he did try to escape, she needed to be certain that he knew exactly what he was entering into. He had already glimpsed her strength, but there were more complex aspects to issuing her a challenge.

"There are specific laws which govern combat with me."

"I can't wait to hear about this." He lifted his arms briefly, then dropped them to his sides. "Enlighten me."

"Anyone who defeats me in hand-to-hand combat becomes my bondmate."

"Bondmate?"

"We'll be pair-bonded under Coalition law."

"What does that mean. Like married?"

"That's a simplification, but an apt one. The laws are part of the agreement between the High Council and the people of Cygnus-1 who supplied the specialized DNA used in my creation. They are a warrior culture, and the Coalition must honor their customs. Pair-bonds are created through martial challenges."

"So if I try to leave and we fight—"

"I will defeat you."

"Or, we'll end up married," he said.

"I will defeat you." She smiled as she imagined how much fun it would be for him to try to best her in battle. "I will also be required to log you among the many who have faced me in combat. It only seems fair I should let you know the ramifications of what you attempt."

He shook his head and turned back to the cliff, his hands on his waist. A small part of her—a ridiculous part—wondered what it would be like should he prevail. The thought was quite distracting.

She almost didn't notice when he quickly shifted his weight away from her, only to bring his arm around in a vicious, back-handed blow. She let the hit partially connect, gauging his strength as she staggered back a few paces.

Unlike most of the Sadirians—and even some challengers of other species she had faced—there was purpose behind his blow that added to his innate strength. He was attuned to his body in a way that most of her challengers had long forgotten.

This was going to be fun. She just needed to be careful not to hurt him.

"Human, you have no idea who you're challenging."

"If you think I'm going to keep playing along with you without a fight, you're mistaken."

"It's you who are mistaken, if you think you stand a chance against me."

"I'm the one who landed the first blow."

"And I shall land the last."

She lashed out with a quick kick, aiming to knock the breath from him to facilitate his recapture. He dodged to the side—which she'd expected. Even at the most basic training level, Sadirian soldiers knew to do their best to avoid getting hit.

As she followed up with two quick punches, he feinted to her right, leaning back so that her attack met nothing but air. An interesting move.

"I've never seen this fighting technique," she said.

"What do you call it?"

"A little bit of this, a little bit of that."

Brendan had warned her that Eric was some kind of Earth soldier. She still couldn't believe their military had such variety on the planet—even among each geographically-based community. "Countries", they were called. And combat training wasn't reserved for soldiers. They permitted their *citizens* to learn.

Foolish.

There was no way that Eric could stand against her strength and durability. She was being cautious, but eventually, she would land a blow that would make him concede. The skimmer was close enough—with its regen bed and med kit—that she was confident she could repair any damage he might sustain. And that was where she needed to get him anyway.

He blocked another kick, but somehow managed to grab her ankle. Instead of trying to hold on to her, giving her leverage she could use in any number of countermoves, he twisted and released it, forcing her to twirl her body in the air to avoid damage to the joint.

She staggered a few paces away when she landed, regaining her balance. What sort of maneuver was that?

Eric stood still, regarding her calmly. He had yet to attack her. Not since that first strike.

She launched herself at him, again with her fists. Perhaps he would get a *little* bit hurt. Except, once more, he stepped to the side—this time striking out and landing a blow to her back that sent her stumbling.

Fun. Yes.

Also infuriating.

She wheeled around, letting go of her control even more. When he deflected her punch, he grunted, shaking his hand as he quickly backed away. Now he was aware of her strength, her speed, and her increased density.

He was getting closer to the trees, but she didn't think he was trying to run. Perhaps he was trying to maintain a safe distance from the cliff's edge behind them.

"Concede," she said. "Before you're injured."

He rubbed his forearm. "Tell me where Brendan is."

He wasn't running because he was concerned for his friend. An admirable sentiment, and one she could perhaps use to end the conflict.

"I already did," she said. "He's on the *Arbiter*, waiting for you."

"I don't believe you."

The statement shouldn't have riled her like it did, but her vision blurred red around the edges. She had never lied to him. Not once. And he continued to insult her honor by saying otherwise.

She charged him, swinging around in a kick that had little control, but ample strength. He dodged it, his eyes wide as her foot connected with the tree behind him. The trunk fragmented in a satisfying explosion of force, sharp pieces of wooden shrapnel flying through the air.

He barely managed to stumble away as the entire thing fell over. It was still partially attached to its base, leaving it at an angle between them.

At least he was on the side nearer her ship. If she could herd him there and get close enough, the cloak would deactivate and he would see it. Perhaps that would be enough to convince him she spoke the truth.

She could have leapt over the trunk, but she wanted him thoroughly convinced that she was not of his world. Bending down, she put her shoulder under the tree and lifted.

The connecting fibers were stronger than she anticipated, but couldn't match her. With a yell, she tore the tree from its base, lifting it above her head just enough that she could hurl it over the cliff.

She turned back to him, panting, and was gratified by the look of shock on his face.

"You see, Earthling. You are no match for me."

He lifted his arms before him, hands fisted, elbows bent. He widened his stance, weight evenly distributed between each foot. A fighting stance.

She felt her lips pull back from her teeth in a smile. This was a challenge. A full-challenge.

Yes...

"I'm not looking to be your match," he said. "I'm looking for Brendan."

"Then let me take you to him." That would end the chance of Eric being hurt, even if it meant ending their battle.

"I'm not going anywhere with you."

"How can you still not believe me?" She gestured to the furrow in the ground near where she'd thrown the tree. Tightness was building in her chest, confusing emotions rising in her that made her want to break things.

"There are drugs that can make people strong. The tree could have been rotted. Hell, it could have been a fake made of balsa wood. Brendan has the resources to arrange it. This whole thing has been a setup from the beginning."

"A setup?"

"A trick." He shook his head. "Why am I still explaining this to you? No more games, Sorca."

"This has never been a game for me," she said. "Not truly. I haven't tricked you, and to accuse me thus taints what we've experienced together."

"Would you give it a rest already?"

The tightness in her chest erupted in a primal yell as she ran at him. Not holding back, she struck again and again. Each time, he deflected, dodged, or sidestepped her attack. Somehow, he was using her strength against her.

"Sorca, stop. You're out of control."

Why should he care? She screamed again, spinning around with a kick that shattered another tree. This one was much larger than the first, and as it fell, she couldn't escape its low branches.

It didn't matter. She could lift it from her as soon as…

Her thoughts scattered as her body flooded with warning. The ground was moving beneath her. No, the tree was pulling her. Pulling her toward the cliff.

"No," she screamed, clawing at the earth. "Not before I've imprinted!"

She kicked at the tree to try to untangle herself from it, but it was moving too fast. They both went over. As it fell free of her at last, she barely managed to catch her fingers on the edge of the cliff.

Eric stood above her, panting. Blood trickled from a scratch along his cheek. She didn't know if it was from the tree or her attacks. All she remembered was the rage. The despair.

Soon, she wouldn't remember that. Her vision blurred at the thought of the loss of him. Of what they had shared.

"I wanted to remember you," she said.

The earth gave way beneath her grip.

Chapter Seven

Eric threw himself to the ground, grabbing Sorca's wrist as she fell from the cliff. He started to slide over with her, and dug his fingers into the ground as far away from the edge as he could. The earth had been loosened by the *second* tree she had somehow smashed with a single kick.

He hoped he would have time to think about that later. At the moment, he turned all of his focus toward keeping them both from falling onto the rocks below. His shoulder felt like it was dislocating, but he ground his teeth against the pain and pulled, keeping his body as close to the earth as he could.

Please... Please...

He repeated the phrase in his mind until her head was above the edge, then her shoulders. As he rolled over, pulling her on top of him, he finally let out a breath.

Damn, she was heavy.

She would probably kill him now. He was vulnerable, his shoulder was sending arcs of pain through his body. With her unbelievable strength, all she'd have to do was punch him hard enough and that would be it.

Instead of picking up the berserker rage that had so clearly taken her over earlier, she straddled him, pushing herself up with her hands on his chest. Gently, thank God.

Finally, she was panting as well. Now he had an idea of what it took to wind her. He wasn't sure if it was adrenaline, fear, or exertion. He was betting on the first. Her eyes were wide and her full lips parted.

"You saved me," she said.

"Yeah."

He struggled to catch his breath. Maybe she wasn't going to kill him after all. She could still be planning to drag him back to her spaceship.

Christ, was he really thinking that was possible? He didn't know what to believe at this point.

"You *risked yourself* to save me."

"It's becoming something of a habit."

She snapped her mouth shut, eyes blazing with intention.

Here it came. What the hell would it be this time?

"I concede," she said.

He wasn't sure he'd heard her right. She had him at a complete disadvantage—at her mercy. Feeling her legs on either side of his thighs, her hips pressing down against his dick, for a brief moment, that didn't seem like the worst thing in the world.

He shook himself internally, remembering the stakes. Either Brendan had been flipped by enemies pretending to be aliens, or…

Or there were aliens invading Earth. One of which—a completely gorgeous one of which—was straddling Eric and gazing down at him with the most intense sense of wonder he'd ever seen.

Shit.

"I'm not marrying you." He spoke mostly to distract himself from the terrifying thought of hostile aliens taking over his planet.

Sorca shook her head. "It's done. You knew the stakes when you challenged me."

"But I didn't defeat you."

"You did. I would be dead if not for you. According to Coalition law, we are pair-bonded."

"Great."

At least she wasn't planning to kill him. At the moment.

"You're disappointed," she said.

"What? No. I mean…" He shook his head, trying to ignore the heat where their bodies touched.

His system was still flooded with adrenaline from the fight. And the sex.

Damn, he had really stepped in it. Way worse than he'd thought earlier, especially now that he was actually considering that everything she'd told him up to this moment had been the truth.

Apparently, he was crazy now, too. Maybe they *were* a pair.

"As your bondmate, I can assist you with your interactions with the Coalition," she said. "I will either resign or retain my commission, depending on what you deem most beneficial."

"Hold on. First, I would never ask any partner to give up something they love for a relationship—and I sure as hell wouldn't make the decision for them. Second, we aren't bondmates."

"We are," she said. "I don't understand why the idea upsets you. I'm considered very valuable—"

"Stop. Just stop. Do you even realize how that sounds? You are your own person, Sorca. No matter where you're from or who...made you."

Genetic engineering. Forced sterilization. And she had mentioned 'remembering him through death'. What the hell did that mean? What kind of life was she leading on that ship? Suddenly, the idea of them being married wasn't looking so bad to him, if it meant he could help get her away from that.

"Marriage is a big deal on my...homeworld," he said.

It felt ridiculous to say those words and mean them. At the same time, thinking back on everything that had happened since they met, it was starting to sound more real —to *feel* more real.

"I won't stand in the way of you...marrying...according to your traditions," she said. "We're only pair-bonded in the Coalition. And many citizens actually enter into a multibond with others. Those are usually more business-oriented mergers, but I imagine they sometimes lead to physical and emotional attachment. You're free to marry whatever Earthling you wish. I do hope that we can occasionally meet to have sex, however."

He would love to have sex with her way more than occasionally. But the rest of what she was saying set his teeth on edge.

"That isn't how we do things on Earth."

"You don't bond with multiple mates or partners?"

"Well, some Earthlings do, but not me. I want a life-partner. One. Someone I can laugh with and care for. Someone who will support me and that I can support. Who understands my need to protect others or maybe even shares it. Someone who understands that there are greater needs out there than our own."

Even as he was saying the words, he realized the truth. The truth she'd been telling him all along, but that sounded too impossible to believe.

With a beaming smile, she said, "I believe I can fulfill all of those criteria."

"Oh, hell."

He grabbed her wrists and pulled her against his chest, then rolled both of their bodies a bit further from the edge of the cliff. His intention had been... He wasn't sure what. But once he was on top of her, seeing her smile up at him with what looked dangerously like hope mixed with excitement, his brain stopped cooperating.

Maybe that tree she dropped on his head had given him a concussion. Maybe this whole thing was some sort of nervous breakdown from working too much.

Work. Right.

He pulled out his handcuffs. With her not resisting him, it was probably the only chance he was going to get to stop this weird situation from spiraling any further into crazyland. He rose so he was straddling her, then pulled her hands into his lap.

"Oh, excellent." She reached for the fastener of his jeans.

"That's not what—"

He let out a sigh, then snapped the handcuffs on her wrists. She held them above her face, cocking her head to the side as she examined them.

"They're beautiful." She beamed up at him. "I accept your gift."

"Those are handcuffs."

She stared at him.

"I'm detaining you. Until I have a better understanding of what's going on."

"So, we're not having sex again?" She sat up so that their chests pressed together, looping her arms behind his neck. "Because these could make that interesting."

His dick jerked at the thought, wanting to be buried in her heat again. Damn, it was tempting. But he needed answers.

"I have questions," he said.

"Ask me whatever you want." She nuzzled his neck. "If it's within my power to answer and won't endanger you, I'll respond."

"And if it betrays the secrets of your people? Of your rank and role on the *Arbiter?*"

"Telling you military secrets of the Coalition without authorization would absolutely endanger you. It would necessitate a mind-wipe." She leaned back and smiled at him. "But if you return to the *Arbiter* with me and join the Department of Homeworld Security, I have no doubt that General Serath will share ample information with you."

"The Department of what, now?"

"Homeworld Security. That's the name Brendan has established for Earth's first contact committee."

Eric let out a laugh and shook his head. "You do realize how impossible this all sounds, right? It's like something out of one of Brendan's sci-fi books."

"Sci-fi. I have heard him say this word repeatedly, as well as General Serath's Earthling-wife, Evelyn."

"Yeah… You might want to get used to it."

The urge to kiss her was strong, but so were other urges. If he started them down that path, he didn't know if he'd have the willpower to stop.

Reluctantly, he extracted himself from her embrace and stood. He offered her his hand to help her up—not that she needed it. She could uproot full-grown oaks and hurl them like javelins, for crying out loud. And this was his…wife?

He could practically hear Brendan's voice teasing him in his head. *"Your* space-*wife."*

Eric growled internally at the thought.

As soon as she was on her feet, she stretched, pulling her hands apart. The chains connecting the handcuffs broke, some of the links flying into the grass.

"What the hell?"

"I'm so sorry, Eric." She looked at him with a deep frown on her face, holding her arms out for him to see the dangling chains. "I've broken your gift. I didn't think they were so fragile and my body is still filled with residual adrenaline."

"It's okay," he said, though he was actually reeling.

Part of him was still in denial. Part that broke along with those handcuffs. She hadn't even been *trying* to break them. How strong was she?

"I wanted to use them the next time we had sex." She sounded genuinely disappointed.

He let out a half-laughing, half-choking sound. "I can always get another pair."

"Excellent." She smiled, then took his hand in hers.

This entire situation was absurd. But he couldn't deny what he'd seen with his own eyes. She was an alien. And that meant…they were married.

If he'd thought for a moment that she could possibly be

telling him the truth, he would never have challenged her, knowing what was at stake. And yet—since he was too far down the rabbit hole to turn back now—being married to a member of the alien race that was supposedly allying itself with Earth had to be a good thing for his planet. Right?

He would do his best to ensure it was. With a sigh, he shook his head, and then said something he never dreamed he would say.

"Take me to your leader."

Chapter Eight

Delight surged within Sorca. Eric was accepting her—accepting the truth about her mission. He *believed* her. Or was starting to.

"I'll take you to my ship, but we must wait until nightfall to depart," she said. "The protocols exist for a reason, and will help to keep us safe."

"Safe from what?"

"As I said, Earth is being invaded by hostile aliens."

"Right. Where are they from?"

"Tau Ceti."

"And you?"

"I am a product of Sadr-4, genetically engineered to serve as a soldier."

"Is that why you're so strong?"

She shook her head. "Not entirely. I'm a Cygnian hybrid —made from Sadirian DNA combined with that of the sentients of Cygnus-1. The Cygnians have incredible strength and durability due to gravity fluctuations on their homeworld."

"Gravity fluctuations?"

"It's near the black hole Earth scientists call Cygnus X-1."

"I'm having trouble wrapping my head around all of this."

She was having her own difficulties believing the reality of her new situation. When he could easily have ended her life during his challenge, Eric had endangered himself to save her. That was *twice* that he had done so in the brief time since they had met. She wondered if there was something in his genetic makeup that compelled him to help others.

And he was her bondmate. A thrill of excitement raced down her spine at the thought. She knew she met his criteria for a fully pair-bonded partner—a wife. All she needed was time in which to convince him.

He didn't believe things easily. He was wary of his opponents and his circumstances. Now that she had more at stake, she might have to give that a try.

Death had never seemed like a big deal to her. But this could be the last physical form she inhabited. She doubted the Coalition would provide Eric with a new version of her if she should die before him.

And if they did create a new version of her, but didn't let her update her imprint beforehand, she would forget Eric and his challenge. Everything they had shared would be lost.

Suddenly, the cliff edge seemed too close.

"Come," she said. "We need to reach my ship as quickly as possible."

"Why? I thought we couldn't leave until tonight."

"That's true. However, I need to log your victory immediately."

"Listen, Sorca—"

She grabbed his wrist and pulled him into step beside her. "It's better for your world." Eventually—she hoped—she could prove that it was the best for him as well.

"This is a cultural misunderstanding."

"It's Coalition law. I'm considered Cygnian, even though the Sadirians created me. Part of the pact between my people and theirs that enables them to use our advanced DNA is that they honor our customs—and the martial challenge is our most sacred tradition. The High Council won't go against this outcome once it is officially logged."

But *only* if it was officially logged.

"Transmissions are currently restricted," she said. "But the ship can be set to automatically send the signal as we depart this evening."

"I haven't agreed to go with you."

The skimmer wasn't far from where they had fought. The space between the cliff's edge and the trees widened, forming the clearing where she had landed.

"You asked me to take you to Brendan." She stepped closer to her ship, setting off the proximity sensor. "This is the only way to reach him."

The cloak fell away, revealing the sleek lines of her personal skimmer.

"Holy…" Eric's voice trailed off.

Sorca let out a breath that purred in her chest as she looked at her ship. She couldn't help it.

In the dark void of space, the black hull of the skimmer was nearly invisible, even without its cloak. On Earth, sunlight gleamed along its surface. Green trees and blue sky reflected on its polished hull.

The curved shadow it cast on the ground would make a pleasant resting space. She wondered if Eric would be willing to have sex with her again now that they were pair-bonded. It seemed an inviting place for it…

"I hope that this addresses any doubts you may still have." She turned to Eric, her smile faltering when she saw him.

His eyebrows were drawn together on his forehead, several furrowed lines between them. A muscle twitched beneath his beard and up along his cheek. His lips were pulled down in a grimace.

She tried to name the emotions flitting across his features. Rage. Fear. Determination.

"Everything you've said is true," he said.

"Yes. I told you that."

"I have questions. Many, many questions."

Sorca nodded curtly, a form of almost-salute she had only ever used with Serath. In that moment, Eric was so like her commanding officer, she couldn't believe she'd not seen the similarities before—primarily the force of will both men seemed to project.

But instead of stalking toward her ship, as Serath would, Eric deferred to her. He gestured to the ship and waited for her to approach first. She walked to the skimmer and pressed her hand against the control that would lower the ramp, watching Eric's expression darken further. This time, she was the one who gestured for him to go first.

Without hesitating, he walked up the short ramp that led to her small vessel. She followed quickly, leaving the ramp open to allow them fresh air. All of the viewports on the ship were open as well.

Eric's gaze scanned every surface of the ship—the controls at each station along the walls, the ladder and hatch leading up to the compact sleeping quarters above, the edges of the rectangular lockers where supplies and weapons were stored.

He looked at the trees through the main viewport. She left him to it, quickly accessing the communications station and setting it to transmit the change in her status as soon as possible.

His silence became unnerving.

"I don't understand why seeing my ship has upset you so," she said. "It proves to you that everything I've said is true. That Brendan is safe."

"He's safe for now. But the fact that you've been telling

me the truth also means that my entire planet is in horrible danger."

"The Coalition will protect Earth from—"

"The Coalition *is* the threat," he nearly yelled. He shook his head, and said, "I'm sorry. Tell me more about your government. Please."

Not their weapons. Not their technology. She was so surprised, she wasn't sure how to respond.

Navigating Eric's cultural mores was proving to be more challenging than she'd anticipated. For once, she actually wished she had spent more time with Vay during the mission's cultural indoctrination session. It might have helped Sorca understand how to communicate with him better.

"Could you narrow your parameters?" she said.

"You said you were designed by your government to be a soldier. Do they design everyone or just the military?"

"Everyone is the product of genetic engineering, designed for a specific societal function."

"Are the results always what they expect?"

"No. Occasionally, citizens don't meet their intended specifications. We call them glitches."

He winced at the word, and his expression hardened. "Are these individuals assigned new roles in your society?"

"Based on their scores on the ability tests we all take after emerging from our maturation chambers, yes."

"How old are they when they emerge?"

"By Earth standards, you would consider them in their early teens."

"Shit," he muttered. He ran a hand over his face briefly. "What happens after they emerge?"

"Everyone continues their development and begins training on basic functioning and societal protocols. Their scoring determines where they're assigned. Most often—especially in cases where their appearance or physicality is not considered within norms—glitches are placed in the military."

Eric's eyebrows hiked up his forehead and his mouth dropped open. He shook his head, and let out a harsh laugh.

"Let me get this straight. Your government takes all the marginalized citizens in your society, and puts them in the military?"

Sorca shrugged. "Specific ships can be designed to accommodate larger people. If a citizen can't properly maneuver in the limited space allowed in the standard Sadirian space station, ship, or dome-world, it isn't possible for them to live among civilians. They serve our society by acting as our peacekeepers and enforcers."

"So, they're your police as well as your military?"

"It's more efficient to have only one segment of the population with this training and equipment."

He shook his head. "I've dealt with many kinds of governments. Democracies, dictatorships—the corrupt, inept, and just plain evil. I have never encountered outright stupid, though. And that is the dumbest thing I have ever heard in my life."

She felt an emptiness within her. Her conditioning mandated that she defend her government, even if the words felt hollow.

"The Coalition has existed for thousands of years," she said.

Existed. Not thrived.

"Your Coalition has devalued an entire segment of its population by labeling them as *glitches*—and then given them access to their most powerful weapons and training."

"Do not underestimate the High Council, Eric. They will do anything to make sure the Coalition remains in control of the galaxy."

"The *galaxy?*" he said. "How many people are we talking about?"

"Including all fully assimilated species—septillions."

"Only septillions?"

"I don't understand."

"The galaxy is a huge place. Why aren't there more people in the Coalition?"

"More aren't needed."

He looked as though she'd struck him. His breath rushed from him as he covered his face with his hands.

"I don't understand your reactions," she said. "Why create more people than you need? Why waste resources?"

He wheeled around and dropped his arms to his sides.

His voice boomed off the walls of the small space they shared. "Because, Sorca, people aren't just resources. They're *people*."

He included everyone in that word. She could feel it with sudden and shocking clarity.

He would consider the needs of Sadirians equal to those of Lyrians, Centaurans, Antareans, Cygnians. Even the loathsome Tau Ceti. She could feel the strength of his words, that he would include all sentients in that one powerful word.

People.

Chapter Nine

The room—ship—was starting to spin. At least, that was how it felt to Eric.

What the fuck kind of messed up society was Sorca from? And these were the "good guys" out to protect Earth?

Yeah. Right.

The enormity of it made him sick to his stomach. His planet and everyone on it was in even more danger than he'd ever imagined. The differences between the people of his homeworld seemed so small compared to this.

And what about Sorca? If her ultra-controlling government found out that she had bonded to an Earthling, what kind of retaliation could she expect? Eric didn't believe for one second that they would just let her walk away.

They'd already put a self-destruct system inside of her. Who knew if they had a way to trigger it remotely? The thought made his heart pound. He had to protect her.

"Don't send the transmission," he said.

"What do you mean?"

"You can't tell your government that we're pair-bonded."

She bristled, and he reached out to her, grasping her arms and pulling her closer in the near-claustrophobic tightness of the ship. He was going to say something, to explain that he wasn't fighting her bizarre combat-based mating ritual.

Instead, he kissed her.

It wasn't slow and it wasn't gentle. He knew she didn't need those things, and he needed...her. Immediately.

He crushed her against him, hands pulling on her clothes, tongue driving into her mouth. It only took her an instant to match his frenzy, her hands burrowing into his hair and holding him locked against her.

He felt her kick off her shoes and followed suit. Then their clothes practically flew off their bodies, ripping in their haste. He was overwhelmed with the need to touch and keep touching her. He needed more.

The moment they were naked—except for the remains of his handcuffs—he picked her up, relieved that she finally trusted herself enough to wrap her legs around his waist. There was a mostly smooth patch of wall near the ladder that led to a hatch in the ceiling.

He swung her body around toward it, hoping he wouldn't press her up against a control that would be activated by contact with her bare skin. He'd seen how she entered commands into the ship by tapping on what looked like etchings in the walls.

As soon as her back was braced against the metal, he pressed his dick to her core. He was already hard, but her muscles were so strong that it took much more force than he was used to using to drive himself into her.

"Tell me," he gasped. "Tell me if I hurt you."

"You won't hurt me, Earthling."

He let out a tiny chuckle at what was becoming her pet name for him. Then he pushed himself into her, deep.

Every millimeter of flesh that parted for him felt like fireworks erupting through his body. Her core was so wet and tight and...perfect.

To him—for him—she was perfect.

He let himself go, his dick sliding against her flesh in frenzied thrusts, her moans and gasps spurring him on. Her nails dug into his back, pain ringing out and joining into the deafening chorus of *being*, of everything he was feeling, physically and emotionally. Pain and pleasure. They faced them together. At least for this moment.

"Eric," she gasped.

Her back arched off from the wall with enough force to nearly knock him back. He grabbed the ladder to keep himself stable, to give him better leverage to intensify his thrusts. He had never fucked anyone like this before, so wildly, abandoning the veneer of civility to share the primal ecstasy of another's flesh.

He pinned her against the wall, grabbing her thigh to keep them connected safely. Her body clenched his dick hard, her strength flowing through every part of her like a drug. He wanted more.

He hammered his hips against hers. Her core pulsed around him, milking him, pushing him over the edge into the purest sense of abandon he'd ever experienced.

"Yes!" Her scream echoed from the walls.

His vision exploded into stars as his climax joined hers. "God, Sorca," he yelled.

He kept on pounding into her, pulling every ounce of pleasure possible from their connection, keeping them both in the epicenter of bliss for as long as he could until it finally started to fade. At last, he stopped, pinning her to the wall, feeling their bodies' rhythmic communication—their heartbeats pulsing where they were joined.

"That…" She licked her lips, her chest pressing against his in sporadic gasps. "That was amazing."

He hesitated a few moments, but then pulled himself from her body before daring to speak. "You can't send the transmission."

Her smile faltered. Dammit, he wished he had more time, but this had to be settled immediately and there was so much to do. So much ahead of him.

Her gaze grew fierce and he knew he was in trouble. She shoved off from the wall, as he'd expected. The force of it knocked him on his ass. She followed immediately, pushing him down and grabbing his wrists, pinning him to the floor of the ship.

"It isn't that I don't want you," he said.

Her grip on his wrists loosened.

"You said you might relinquish your position in their military. What would happen to you if you did? I don't trust them to let you go."

She sat back on his hips, their bodies comfortably pressing together. She pulled his arms down as she moved, so that his hands rested on her waist.

"The High Council won't risk violating the agreement with Cygnus-1," she said. "If they do, they know they'll never receive new samples of Cygnian DNA. Besides, they only have to wait until I die due to an Earth ailment or age or my own..."

"Impulse control issues?"

The scenarios she presented were hypothetical, but he didn't like even thinking about it. Still, when she grinned this time, he felt as if he was part of the mystery behind the smile. His chest felt full at the realization—knowing it would only make it that much harder for him to walk away.

"*I* am the one who has bonded with you. Once I die, the Coalition can clone me again and reprogram my mind with the latest imprint they have on file from before this assignment. They risk nothing by giving me a single lifetime with you."

He sat up, fast. So fast that they nearly conked heads.

"Clone you *again?* Reprogram you? Holy shit, Sorca, is everybody—"

She covered his lips with her fingertips. "It's only the Cygnian hybrids, as far as I know."

"How many of you are there?"

"I don't know. They don't let us meet."

Of course they didn't.

"I still don't understand how such an oppressive government controls so many people—so many cultures. And you say they maintain peace?"

"*Balance* helps."

He knew he was going to regret asking, but he did it anyway. "And that is?"

"A drug that regulates the mental and emotional states of most citizens. Hence it's name—'balance'. It's meant to maintain equilibrium and keep everyone functioning at maximum efficiency. But it also…dulls the will."

He covered his eyes as she spoke, shaking his head. "I should have guessed."

He dropped his hands back to her hips, preparing to argue further. He doubted Sorca would just go along with him. She was too determined, too passionate for that.

"If they even suspect that they can't replicate you, there's no way they'll let you go." He opened his eyes to hold her gaze with his. "Do you understand? That's why you can't tell them we're pair-bonded."

"I understand your concerns, but it's too late. The transmission has already been logged in the ship. There's no way to stop it."

Chapter Ten

"That doesn't mean I can't help you." Sorca let Eric nudge her aside so that he could rise. She stood with him, trying to make him see reason. "For however long I have —"

"Stop. You don't get it." He paced a few steps away, putting as much distance between them as he could on the small vessel.

"Get what?" She wasn't sure what he was planning to withhold from her. Or why it should matter enough that her breath was catching in her chest.

He let out a deep sigh. "You say we're married according to your ways. I'm not going to try to get out of that."

She couldn't believe his words. Was he actually accepting her as a bondmate? Fully?

"It was my error in judgment that put us in this situation," he said.

"Error." Her heart felt leaden. Her vision grew red around the edges as the extreme sways in emotion took their toll.

If he thought their pair-bonding was a mistake, there was no way he would ever truly accept her. She would be a tool for him, just as she'd been for the Coalition all of her life. At least it was a familiar role.

"Then tell me how I can be of greatest use to you." The sharp edge to her tone was new to her ears.

"Partners don't use each other, Sorca. That's what I'm trying to tell you." He crossed back to her, gently gripping her arms. "I don't want to use you. I want to help you."

"*You* want to help *me*? But, I'm supposed to—"

"So am I. I can see it in you. It's what we both do. We serve. We protect. But have you ever stopped to think that maybe you need protection as well? The Coalition has exploited you. Exploits all of their populace from the sounds of it."

"It's all we've known." She couldn't begin to imagine another life. Except...

Except, she already had. She had already been creating scenarios where she remained on Earth with Eric. She could find a way to contribute—especially with their shared abilities and military training. She would ease his life with her presence. They would spend their days together bringing peace to his people, and their nights sharing their bodies, bringing peace to each other.

The idea of it was frivolous and dangerous. It could only bring disappointment, such as she was feeling in that moment. There was no way she could attain that life.

"I don't want to use you," he said.

"Then you do not wish to be my bondmate."

"I didn't say that."

"Then what *do* you want, Eric?"

He stared at her, the muscle along his jaw twitching again. "I want my planet to be safe. I want my people—all of my homeworld's people—to find a way to get along. And I don't want to be at the mercy of a soulless dystopian government for its survival."

She shook her head. "I can't give you any of those things. But as long as you strive for them, I can promise to be at your side."

"Is that what *you* want? If you could do anything in the world—anything in the universe, I should say—what would you do?"

No one had ever asked her that question. No one asked anyone that question in the Coalition.

"If you knew that you had *time*, Sorca. If you weren't so okay with being...replaced with an exact duplicate. What would you want?"

"I would want to spend that time with you."

"You've only just met me."

"I believe I've learned a great deal about who you are in that time. You've risked yourself to save me multiple times. You've gone along with what you thought was a game—first to support your friend, I suppose, and then to try to help him. You're both playful and serious, and can be as impulsive as I, while never abandoning your mission."

The more she considered it, the more traits they seemed to share. The physical compatibility alone would have been enough for her, but she believed they could eventually forge a true emotional connection. Like the one between Serath—Adam—and Evelyn.

"I think we're a good match, Eric Peterson. I will make your mission mine and protect Earth at your side. I will protect those who you care about and...hope to someday be counted among them."

"You already are."

Her heart seemed to swell in her chest, her ribs enduring a pressure unlike anything she'd experienced. She felt... full.

"You're talking about giving up the galaxy to stay here with me," he said.

"It's not that much of a sacrifice."

He laughed and shook his head. His eyes darkened as his pupils dilated. Was the thought of staying with her that stimulating to him? She shifted a bit closer, tilting her lips toward his.

When he spoke, his tone was serious again, his breath warm on her skin. "I need to talk to your commanding officer. And I need to know that Brendan is okay."

"I swear to you that he is safe."

"I believe you. I'll just feel better when I see him with my own eyes."

"Night will fall shortly. I can answer more of your questions in the meantime."

"Let's start with these 'hostile aliens' invading Earth. You called them the Tau Ceti?"

"Yes." She tried to mask the disdain she felt for them from her voice.

"What do they want? Territory? Resources?"

"So far, all we have determined is that they are…feeding on the populace."

His eyes widened. "They're eating people?"

"Not all of them."

"Not…" He sputtered. "What parts are they leaving behind?"

"I'm being unclear. Their genetic engineers have altered the base physiology of the Tau Ceti so that they are capable of biting a human and drawing out blood, siphoning out chemicals that give the Tau Ceti a feeling of wellbeing, and returning the blood to their target."

His expression was oddly devoid of emotion. He looked almost as though he'd been stunned. Perhaps he still didn't understand. She struggled to find words that would assist him.

"Brendan has been calling them, 'vampire space frogs'."

"Vampire space frogs," Eric repeated. "I'm just…going to give my subconscious some time to work on that. How are the humans affected by the attack?"

"Most likely they suffer from chemical imbalances

afterwards. And the Tau Ceti must perform some sort of mind-wipe on them, which would be disorienting at the least."

He let out a breath. "Like we don't have enough problems already. Why don't the Tau Ceti just take that drug the Coalition is using to control the rest of the populace?"

"The Tau Ceti are one of the few sentient species whose physiology is incompatible with *Balance* and *Coupling*," she said.

"*Coupling*—the other drug… I probably shouldn't ask, but what does that one do?"

"It takes the body through the stages of sexual arousal through climax."

He snorted and shook his head. "Drugs instead of sex."

"Or in addition to. Many citizens choose to take *Coupling* with a partner to increase its effectiveness in providing emotional fulfillment. Having now experienced…" She struggled again to find the best word to express her thought.

"The real thing?" he suggested.

She smiled. "Indeed. Having now experienced 'the real thing', I can state that it's not at all effective in providing a true sense of emotional or even physical connection."

"And what will the High Council do once others in the Coalition start to hear rumors about what Brendan and his…bondmate have experienced? Or this General of yours and his Earth partner? Are we going to be overrun by Sadirians looking for Earth mates?"

She had to laugh at that thought. "Not at all. Earth is a designated preservation planet. It's exceedingly difficult to gain authorization to come here, and there must be a compelling reason to do so."

At least, there should have been. With the arrest of the planetary liaison and the presence of the Tau Ceti, she had a feeling that perhaps more was going on planetside than even General Serath knew.

The crease appeared between Eric's brows that she had noted correlated with his experience of strong emotion. This time, he seemed deep in thought as well.

After a few moments, Eric said, "With how controlling the High Council is about everything, how is it they didn't know about the Tau Ceti presence?"

"We have recently discovered that Earth's planetary liaison was corrupt. At the very least, he's been smuggling items offworld to accumulate resources—most likely with the help of the Tau Ceti. Several high-level members of the Coalition have been arrested in conjunction with our investigation."

"Has anyone questioned this liaison yet?"

"I have. I'm the head of security for the Coalition's flagship, remember?"

He smiled at her softly. "That's right, you are. It sounds like an important position."

"It is."

He was still holding onto her arms and began rubbing his thumbs back and forth across her skin, causing the follicles to stand on end in that stimulating way. The motion seemed instinctual to him, as if he didn't even have to think to provide her with pleasure and comfort.

"You're offering to give up a lot to help Earth," he said.

"To help *you*. But yes, Earth will benefit as well."

"Did you discover anything useful from the liaison?"

"When I was questioning him, my priority was to find conspirators within the Coalition. I wasn't thinking of your world or people. If Serath allows it, I'll question the liaison again with this in mind."

"Do you think Serath will let me be present?"

"That depends on whether you join the Department of Homeworld Security or not."

Eric let out a little laugh. "Brendan must be having the time of his life with this."

"Actually, he takes the entire situation quite seriously. He's convinced the matter is more serious than we know, and has theorized that any number of your...'urban legends' are actually rooted in extra-terrestrial activity on the planet."

"Alien sewer-gators. Great."

"He hasn't mentioned 'sewer-gators', but he has speculated about beings known as Grays, the Yeti, and Bigfoot."

Eric lowered his head. His shoulders trembled, as if these names had frightened him.

"Don't be afraid," she said. "I'll protect you from any alien incursion—"

He started to laugh, lifting his face to hers with a tense smile crossing his features. "I'm sorry. The absurdity of it all is just getting to me."

"There is nothing to apologize for. You've assimilated a great deal of information quite well in an extremely short period of time."

"I'm glad you feel that way, because I think I need a little time to let my brain process this all."

"Understandable. If it would assist you…" She leaned even closer, until her breasts brushed against his chest. "I'd be happy to engage in a distracting activity."

His smile softened as he lowered his lips to hers, and murmured, "Bondmates with benefits."

Chapter Eleven

Outside of the ship, the view was amazing. Eric gave himself a few moments alone to watch the sunset and try to get his thoughts in order while Sorca prepped the ship for departure. He was about to leave the planet. *The planet.*

Part of him still wondered if this was part of some elaborate hoax that Brendan had put together. He had the money—and motive—to build the ship. He could have created replicas of trees rigged to look like Sorca was knocking them down during the fight. But Sorca herself...

She's what had convinced Eric that it was all true. She was just too real.

There was a rawness to her that he had originally mistaken for instability. Now that he knew more about her history and her culture, he understood better.

If he had died repeatedly and been recreated as the product of cloning and memory implants—and had more of the same to look forward to... He wasn't sure he'd be handling that as well as she was. She was even stronger than he'd realized.

Earth was in danger. It was a huge responsibility to be

one of the few people who knew about that. But Sorca was in danger, too. And the threat to her felt much closer. The need to protect her was a hell of a lot more immediate and tangible than invading aliens he had yet to see.

He heard rustling behind him. Sorca was in the ship—on the other side of the clearing. The hair on the back of his neck stood on end as he slowly turned, his thoughts of aliens making his imagination run wild.

A deer was standing at the edge of the treeline. Just a deer.

He was about to laugh, but he still had that feeling of misgiving. The deer took a step closer. Its hide was pale. Was it the same gray deer from earlier?

Eric had asked Sorca about the Tau Ceti's appearance. Apparently, they had engineered themselves to look like Sadirians, which meant they also looked like a regular human. Well, right up until they snapped down the fangs embedded in the roof of their mouths before feeding.

She hadn't mentioned anything about aliens that looked like deer. This was probably just a wild animal, which was dangerous enough on its own. He took a step back, then remembered that the cliff's edge was a few feet behind him, along with a sixty-foot drop that ended in jagged rocks.

"Easy," he said.

The deer stepped into the clearing, its head low to the ground. It seemed docile enough. Far more docile than it had any reason to be. It glanced over at the ship. Maybe there was something about the skimmer that was making it behave strangely?

It sped up as it approached Eric with more purpose. What the purpose was, he had no idea. He stayed still, arms out to his sides in what he hoped was a reassuring gesture.

The deer stopped right in front of him. It was bigger than he'd expected. Hunting animals wasn't something he'd ever had an interest in, so his experience was limited. He had enough of tracking things down in his work.

"Easy," he said again.

He held his breath as the deer cocked its head to the side, staring at him. Its pupils were dilated, entirely obscuring its irises. Now that he thought about it, its eyes seemed bigger than they should.

"This is just too weird."

The deer's lips quirked up, almost like it was amused. Eric must be worse off than he thought.

It lurched up on its hind legs. Eric lifted his arms to defend himself. He'd seen videos of deer attacking hunters before, and expected it to start lashing out at him with its forelegs. Instead, the deer started to glow.

"What the hell?"

Through the silver light emanating from it, he saw its eyes grow bigger—still entirely black. Its head shortened and rounded, its ears retreating into its scalp. Its limbs and torso lengthened to slender, sinuous reeds.

Holy shit.

The transformation happened so fast. It looked like a Gray—the alien most commonly described by humans Eric *used* to think were crackpots. He would never discount a report of a UFO sighting again.

Partially blinded, he didn't see when the thing lashed out with one of its oddly moving arms, wrapping its long fingers around Eric's neck and squeezing. He couldn't breathe, couldn't call for help. He grabbed the Gray's wrists, trying to break free, but the thing wouldn't budge.

Still glowing dimly, the Gray lifted Eric off of the ground, pulling him closer. Its mouth was a thin slit in a vaguely featureless face, but he swore the corners of the lipless gash twitched up in a smile. With its free arm, it pointed at Eric's face, its sharply pointed finger getting closer and closer.

Please don't probe me...

It grabbed the edge of Eric's mouth, sliding its finger along his cheek and teeth, like it was doing a DNA swab test. If he could have moved his neck in the thing's iron grip, he would have bitten it, but he was too busy holding himself up, trying to suck in any amount of air so he didn't black out.

The Gray pulled his finger from Eric's mouth, then... licked it. It cocked its head to the side, like the deer had done.

What the fuck?

The light grew brighter again, and Eric could feel the

thing's hand changing shape around his neck. It shrank down to a more average human size. The moment Eric's feet touched the ground, he dug his thumb into its forearm in a spot that would cause a human to reflexively open their hand.

The Gray dropped him and he rolled as he hit the ground. Eric wasn't sure if he'd escaped or the thing had released him. All he cared about was the fresh air burning its way across his bruised windpipe and into his lungs.

Gasping, he looked up to see the woman from the diner that Sorca had tried to talk to about copulation protocols. The woman's eyes were completely black and her features half-way between the Gray's and a human's.

As he watched, its features shifted again, losing the definition they had just gained. Then, it swelled larger as it coalesced into a familiar shape and face—*his*. The light dimmed, and Eric was left staring at an exact duplicate of himself.

With all the classified projects he'd worked on, he could think of dozens of reasons that someone would want to copy and replace him. But he had a feeling this alien was after something less Earth-based.

The Gray grinned at him, then reached down and started dragging Eric to his feet with inhuman strength. He doubted it was a compassionate gesture. This close to the cliff's edge, it was almost certainly just trying to push him over before he regained his voice.

Eric pretended to wobble on his feet, coiling his strength and "stumbling" closer to the Gray. As soon as he was in a good enough position, he launched his shoulder into the thing's chin with all his strength.

The Gray was taken by surprise and staggered back from the blow. Eric was about to press his advantage when he heard Sorca call out from the ship.

"Don't move," she said. "Either of you."

He turned to see her standing at the end of the ramp with what was obviously some kind of high-tech rifle braced against her shoulder—and aimed in his direction. In unison, he and the Gray raised their hands.

"Sorca, it's me," the Gray said. Its voice perfectly matched Eric's.

"No, *I'm* me," Eric said.

"I don't know what that thing is. It attacked me and somehow turned into me."

"It's a Gray," Eric said. "I don't know what you call them, but that's their name on Earth."

"Sorca, you told me the only aliens on Earth are the Sadirians and the Tau Ceti," it said. "What *is* this thing?"

Shit, how did it know that those were the only aliens Sorca had told Eric about? Unless it had been following them and listening in on everything.

He'd noticed the weird deer while Sorca was carrying him to the ship—when she'd started telling him about the dangers Earth faced. And if it *had* been the lady from the diner, it could have been following them the whole time. It could have seen the results of their fight, and heard them talking afterwards.

"Sorca, please trust me," it said. "I'm your bondmate."

And there it was. This thing was after Sorca.

Chapter Twelve

"Describe what you saw." Sorca kept the phase rifle pointed at the two Erics in front of her. Not many sentients could alter their appearance. The situation was bad. She just wasn't sure *how* bad.

"It was tall, thin, and gray-skinned," the Eric on her left said.

Right-Eric chimed in as well. "And had dark black eyes. Huge eyes. And slender limbs."

Cygnus X. The situation was dire indeed.

"You're describing a Scorpiian. They're bounty hunters and deadly assassins." She watched both Erics' reactions. Neither flinched at being identified. Both looked equally surprised.

But what was a Scorpiian doing on Earth?

Though she hadn't sent her transmission yet, her ship was receiving data from the *Arbiter*. Apparently, Khel had already returned to the ship with Brendan's sister, Paige.

They'd sent an emergency transmission to her ship to let her know that the Tau Ceti had been setting up spawning pools on Earth—a scenario Sorca would never have imagined.

The Tau Ceti were facing extreme sanctions for these acts, but the information she received hinted at some kind of new technology they'd developed that must have made that prospect less upsetting for them. It also made them a much greater threat to the Coalition—and Earth.

She hadn't told Eric yet, but there were supposedly Centaurans on Earth as well. Who knew how many other sentients had invaded the planet or what their plans for it might be. She needed to determine which of these Erics was *her* Eric and dispatch the Scorpiian so they could get to the *Arbiter* as quickly as possible.

"I'm guessing you mean someone from one of the Scorpii systems," left-Eric said.

Some*one*, not some*thing*. The probability that left-Eric was the true Eric increased.

"She sure as hell isn't talking about the bug," right-Eric said.

Hmm. The humor on that one…

"Sorca, if that weapon can stun us, shoot us both. It's the only way we can assure your safety," left-Eric said.

"Unless it wants you to do so," right-Eric said. "What if there's more than one and it's trying to get you alone?"

Right-Eric was both displaying his concern for her and his ignorance. Scorpiians always worked by themselves. That way, they didn't have to share their bounties when they captured their targets.

But what bounties could it be seeking on Earth? If it tried to collect on a bounty, it would have to admit to trespassing on a preservation planet. Unless it was a covert bounty or...

Or sanctioned at an extremely high level. Perhaps even by the High Council itself. Which would mean that they were already aware that Earth was being invaded.

She set aside that truly disturbing thought. It was essential that she navigate this situation successfully. She had to warn General Serath. And she had to save Eric. Whichever one of these versions was truly him.

"Scorpiians are immune to the stun function of this phase rifle," she said. "As one of you well knows. Stunning you both would make an ambush that much easier, and remove my only support personnel."

"Support personnel?" right-Eric said. "I thought I was more than that to you."

Her heart gave a little lurch. Before she could respond, left-Eric spoke out.

"It knows everything that's passed between us. *Everything.* Including the fact that we're pair-bonded. It's after you. It wants to use you, through our bond."

That was a terrifying thought. If she ended up with the Scorpiian without knowing it, it could use her position and status to its own ends. Scorpiians were masters at manipulation.

"Lock us both up in the sleeping chamber of the

skimmer," left-Eric said. "Surely the people on the *Arbiter* can tell us apart when we get there."

"How do you know so much about her ship?" right-Eric said.

"Because she told me, dumbass."

Sorca grinned. Both had humor. Both looked exactly like her Eric. But which one was he?

"It would be much too dangerous to bring a Scorpiian aboard the *Arbiter*," she said. "We'll have to resolve this between the three of us."

"Great." Right-Eric rolled his eyes.

"How does the Scorpiian know so much about us?" she said.

Right-Eric replied first. "It's been following us in the form of a deer—a common woodland animal in this area. I saw it while you were carrying me up the hillside, but I didn't say anything because I didn't think it was important."

"And it saw me see it," left-Eric said. "But it did a piss-poor job of imitating a deer, because its hide was way too *gray*."

Left-Eric was trying to goad right-Eric. The tactic seemed to be in line with what she knew of her new bondmate. Right-Eric didn't show any reaction to the insult.

From what left-Eric said, there weren't many questions she could ask to establish his identity. She didn't know much about him yet. She was determined to get through this and have the opportunity to learn more.

"This will get us nowhere," she said. "If the Scorpiian has truly overheard everything, there's no way that talking can determine who is the imposter and who is truly Eric."

"Do you have something else in mind?" left-Eric said.

"Only one person has ever bested me in combat. If we fight, I'll know who the real Eric is."

"No, no, no," right-Eric said. "That's way too dangerous."

Left-Eric shook his head. "I agree. There has to be another way."

Sorca locked the rifle and set it down on the ramp. "There is no other way. And be advised, I will only be able to identify you correctly by not holding back. I expect you both to do the same."

"Sorca," left-Eric said.

There was no time to waste, with the sun setting and stars knew how many hostiles planetside. She looked from one of them to the other and grinned.

This was going to be fun.

With a battle cry, she ran toward the pair of them, attempting to backhand the one on the left while spinning into a kick aimed at the right. Both men leapt out of range, as she expected. They mirrored each other's stances perfectly.

Scorpiians were feared for good reason. They were

masters of infiltration, getting close to their bounties before springing their attacks. She couldn't let her guard down. At the same time, she didn't want to hurt the real Eric.

She followed up her attack first with the Eric who had started out on her right. Kicks and punches that he parried easily enough. Despite what she'd said, she was holding back, which probably wasn't the best course of action to determine who was the imposter.

She increased the force of her blows. Right-Eric was still able to block them. He even managed to land a few hits that she'd be feeling when the adrenaline rush of the battle was over.

During her attack, she had left her back open. Left-Eric hadn't taken advantage of that. Then again, the Scorpiian could easily have predicted that Eric wouldn't be eager to fight her.

She sprinted toward left-Eric, but instead of engaging with her, he...ran away. Not far, but all he did was try to stay out of her reach.

He hadn't seemed the type to run before. Perhaps this was the imposter.

"I won't fight you, Sorca," left-Eric said. "I'm not the Scorpiian."

"That's exactly what it would say." She closed the distance between them and swung at him—still holding back her strength and speed. Which one *was* he? "Engage me. It's the only way I can know for certain."

His lips pressed together in a thin line.

She swung at him again, but this time, he stood his ground, deflecting her blow with that curious fighting technique he'd used before. Yes, this could very well be her Eric. A few more tests would be necessary.

Before she could attack again, the other Eric came up behind him and struck him in the back of the head with the rifle. Left-Eric crumpled to the ground.

"What are you doing?" she yelled.

"I was trying to help you," right-Eric said.

She grabbed the rifle, easily jerking it from his grasp. Her vision clouded with red. What if that was the real Eric bleeding at her feet? But what if *this* was the real Eric?

She dropped the weapon and leapt at him, grabbing his shoulders and pulling him forward so that she could strike him with her forehead. He staggered back from the impact, and she let him, releasing her hold.

Another punch—that she successfully landed. A kick that sent him sprawling to the ground. As soon as he regained his feet, she was on him, no longer holding back.

There were no graceful dodges, no redirecting the energy of her attack. Just the brutal force of her strength and speed pummeling him into a bloody…

No blood. There was no blood.

She looked back at left-Eric, who was struggling to get to his feet, using the rifle to prop himself up. Blood ran down his temple and into the collar of his shirt. Red, human blood, not the quicksilver that ran in a Scorpiian's veins.

How injured was he?

Her skin prickled with fear. She needed to get him to the regen bed.

"Look out!" he yelled.

She turned back to the Scorpiian, just as it morphed its hand into a sharp spike. Dodging it with nanoseconds to spare, she grabbed its arm and pulled it off balance in a clumsy approximation of one of the real Eric's techniques. She caught the Scorpiian before it could fall to the ground, hefting it into the air. The inertia of its attack actually made the process much easier. There was definitely something to this Earth combat.

With another battle cry that drowned out its shrill scream, she ran toward the cliff and tossed it over the edge. She turned back to Eric just as he managed to get to his feet. He took a few wobbly steps in her direction, falling into her arms as he reached her.

Smiling, he said, "Remind me never to piss you off."

Chapter Thirteen

The forest was spinning wildly around Eric as Sorca drew his arm across her shoulders, supporting most of his weight. He felt nauseated and his vision was blurry. Not good. He still managed to keep his grip on the space rifle that his evil twin had cold-cocked him with, though.

He probably had a concussion. At least the Gray—the Scorpiian—was gone.

"Are you okay?" he asked.

"You're the one who can't stand, yet you ask if I'm okay?"

Eric half-shrugged. "That thing hit you pretty hard a couple of times."

"I'm more durable than that, as you well know. I'm more concerned for you. The regen bed in my ship can address your injuries."

"Wait a minute." Something was nagging at the back of his mind—swirly as it was. "The Scorpiian. Did you hear it hit the ground?"

Sorca looked up at him, her eyes wide. She mostly carried him to the edge of the cliff.

The rocks below weren't splattered with carnage, as he'd expected. In fact, there was nothing on them at all.

"Eric."

He followed Sorca's gaze to the treeline beneath them, a hundred yards or so from the bottom of the cliff. The Scorpiian stood there, in its tall, Gray form, with folds of near-transparent skin connecting its arms and legs illuminated by the setting sun.

"Did that thing just glide to safety after being thrown off a cliff?" He wanted to be sure he wasn't imagining things.

"Scorpiians are feared for good reason."

"At least it doesn't look like me anymore."

"Come." She turned them back toward the ship, moving at a fast pace. "We must leave the planet as quickly as possible."

"The sun hasn't quite set yet."

"I want you healed before we board the *Arbiter*. You'll need to be at your best."

"Why do I feel like there's something you're not telling me?"

"Because you're observant and intelligent. And there are several things I haven't told you yet."

A wave of nausea washed over him as he wondered what else could go wrong.

As soon as they were aboard, she closed the ship's ramp. Lights along the ceiling and floor began to glow, immediately replacing the sunlight that had just been cut off. Sorca pressed a control, and a bench slid out of the wall. She set him on it and knelt beside him.

"Are you in much pain?" she said.

"Not really." His head felt like it was cracked in half, but he could deal with that.

"I don't believe you."

She smiled, tracing her fingers over his forehead. He could feel her gently pulling hair free that was sticking to his skin.

"I warned you that you would be injured if you persisted in trying to defend me," she said.

"You're worth it."

Her eyes widened and her mouth dropped open. For a wrenching moment, he was afraid she might start to cry. But not his Sorca. *His* Sorca.

He cupped her jaw, tilting her head up to his so that he could claim her mouth. He delved into her, caressing her tongue with his, feeling her rise up and melt against him. The room was still spinning, but possibly for a much more pleasant reason when they finally parted.

"I'm glad you figured out it was me. And not just because I wouldn't have stood a chance of surviving being chucked off the cliff like that."

"Even in the battle, I could tell you were trying to protect me. It truly is hardwired into your DNA."

He laughed and shook his head. He couldn't deny it. As far back as grade school, he'd felt compelled to help people when they were being picked on. Too bad that sentiment hadn't been passed on to the Scorpiian when it took his shape.

Sorca picked up the rifle and carried it to its storage rack, snapping it into place. The wall slid closed over it, making the weapons locker nearly invisible.

"I think I'll feel better once you teach me how to shoot one of those things," Eric said.

"That time will come sooner than you think." Her hands flew over the etchings on the wall, bringing systems to life throughout the ship.

Lights flickered on the walls, and a gridline superimposed itself over the viewscreen. He could hear things powering up and feel the vibration of engines through his seat.

"Does this thing have seatbelts?" he said.

She turned back to him and smiled. "Our uniforms have safety harnesses built into them that we can attach to the walls in case of sudden gravity loss. We'll want to change before we board the *Arbiter*. It's standard protocol."

"Far be it from me to stand against standard protocol. Are you going to tell me that news before we get there, too?"

"I was going to wait till you were out of the regen bed."

"I'd rather not."

She sighed, then crossed the small space and sat next to him. "The Tau Ceti are much more invested in Earth than we thought. General Serath sent a coded transmission to alert me to the danger. They've been setting up spawning pools—altering Earth's environment so that they could make a permanent home here."

His stomach lurched again. Maybe he *should* have waited till her regen bed fixed his probable-concussion. He rubbed his eyes, trying to clear his mind.

"So what? Sanctions? Arrests? I can't see the Coalition going to war for a planet that's not even one of their members."

"If they go to war, it will not be over this. In fact..."

He'd only seen her censor herself once. What was she holding back this time?

"We're bondmates, remember? And to me, that means we're partners. I want—I *need*—to know what we're dealing with."

She nodded, then said, "I have grave concerns. The fact that there is a Scorpiian bounty hunter operating on Earth leads me to believe..."

Her voice trailed off, a furrow appearing between her eyebrows. He reached over and stroked her cheek.

"Sorca..."

She took a deep breath and let it out slowly. Here it came...

"Scorpiians often work for the High Council. They don't pursue bounties that won't pay out for them. There are no bounties on Earth that they could be seeking that aren't sanctioned, even if they're covert."

"I don't understand."

"I believe that the High Council is aware that there are other sentients trespassing on Earth. They may even be the ones behind the Scorpiian's presence. And if that's the case, they may have been aware of the planetary liaison's actions as well. They might not think there's a problem on Earth at all."

The room spun faster as he processed her words. If their government was aware of its citizens breaking their own laws, and was using secretive ways of dealing with it instead of facing it in the open... Earth faced an even greater challenge than he'd realized.

"Let's get me to the regen bed," he said. "I need to talk to Serath."

Chapter Fourteen

Back aboard the *Arbiter*, Sorca experienced the strange sense of detachment that usually only accompanied adjusting to a new body. She supposed it was a reaction to the knowledge that this was most likely among the last times she would walk these corridors. The adjustment was easier with Eric walking at her side.

"I feel ridiculous," he said.

Another crewmember paused to let them pass, pressing his back to the wall to give them room. The *Arbiter* had larger corridors than most ships in the fleet, but the Coalition still understood that space was to be used as efficiently as possible—just as they used their people.

That knowledge had never chafed as it did now. Earth truly did have a transformative effect. Or at least its inhabitants did.

Eric shook his head. "I can't believe your uniform is a silver catsuit."

"I don't know what cats have to do with it, but our uniforms have been designed to provide maximum protection while utilizing the fewest resources."

"Uh-huh." He walked a bit closer to her when they were alone again, and said, "I do have to admit, you look gorgeous in it."

She grinned at the compliment. "As do you."

He chuckled. "Thanks."

She wished she could wear the special bracelets he'd given her underneath it, but he had convinced her to leave them back in her quarters. Perhaps she could have one of the mechanical engineers aboard the ship repair and reinforce the chain that had connected them...

"I really like the look on your face right now," Eric said.

Grinning, she pressed the control panel that gave her access to Serath's main meeting room. The door slid open, revealing the relatively large, circular space. Eric followed her inside.

Her next-ranking security officer, Ari, stood on the far side of the room, his dark eyes taking in everything. He nodded curtly at Sorca, his bald head nearly brushing the ceiling of the chamber.

Vay stood next to him, her gaze darting around the room. She needed to be trained to be more discrete in her environmental observations.

That task will fall to Ari now...

Brendan was standing on the near side of the oval table that filled most of the chamber. He and Eric walked briskly toward each other and clasped hands, also grasping each other's shoulders.

"I'm glad you could make it," Brendan said.

"Your friend here didn't give me much choice." Eric grinned at her over his shoulder. "She carried me to her ship when I tried to leave."

Brendan took a deep breath and held it for a moment before blowing it out. Visibly attempting to be calm, he said, "Sorca. The next time I ask you to go get someone, please don't *abduct* them."

She shrugged. "Next time, give clearer orders."

"I'm glad she insisted," Eric said. "From what I've learned, things are pretty bad."

"They are much worse than any of us knew." Serath's commanding tone echoed across the room.

He entered with his bondmate, Evelyn. Khel followed with a woman who had the same red hair as Brendan. Sorca guessed this was Paige.

"Please sit," Serath said. "We have much to discuss."

Sorca led Eric around the table so that they could sit across from Brendan and Earth's new planetary liaison, his bondmate, Kira. Everyone's expressions were grim—even the normally cheerful Evelyn's.

She tucked a lock of her blonde hair behind her ear and tried to push a pair of glasses that she was no longer wearing up her nose. After her first sleep in a regen bed, her eyesight was perfect.

Wearing anything on one's face was dangerous on board. If the ship suffered decompression, the helmet built into the collars of their suits would unfold to cover their heads and seal the uniform. Evelyn's glasses would have obstructed the process, but she still seemed to mourn their loss.

Sorca understood a bit better now why Evelyn had yelled at Serath afterwards about not being consulted before her body was altered.

"Kira," Serath said. "Speak."

Kira looked a bit surprised. Her gaze flitted to each person seated around the table. When her eyes locked with Brendan's, he smiled at her and nodded slightly. She immediately looked more comfortable, straightening in her chair

She spoke in a strong voice. "The Tau Ceti very nearly set up spawning pools on Earth. They've been feeding on the population for an undetermined amount of time. There are also Centaurans somewhere on the planet. The previous planetary liaison is in custody on board. We've determined that he was running an extensive smuggling operation that was supported by several very high-level members of the Coalition."

"Sorca," Serath said. "Your report."

He glared at her with his mismatched eyes—one bright blue and the other green. His presence dominated the room. She noted that everyone started to fidget in their seats. Even Eric was affected, sitting straighter in his chair and not taking his eyes off of their leader.

Serath had told her once that she was the only one who seemed to be unaffected by him—which was part of why he valued her so much as his chief security officer. Undoubtedly, he was not happy to know of her pair-bonding.

He'd get over it.

"The High Council itself was most likely aware of the smuggling operation," Sorca said.

"What?" Khel's shout echoed in the room. He had always been extremely loyal to the Coalition. Sorca wondered if his new relationship with the Earthling, Paige, would alter that.

Paige set her hand on his shoulder, and said, "Easy, there. Let's hear her out."

"Present your evidence," Kira said.

Sorca grinned at the new liaison. The woman had a voice like steel. It seemed to match her temperament. Earth was in good hands there. Sorca hoped it would be enough.

"Eric and I were attacked by a Scorpiian," Sorca said.

Most of the Sadirians in the room gasped. Serath's glare darkened.

"How in the name of the Solar Cross are you still alive?" Kira said.

"Um, excuse me?" Evelyn raised her hand tentatively, as she often did when she had something to contribute. "Scorpions aren't that dangerous. Even really big ones. You can just stomp on them. I don't get why it's such a big deal."

Brendan and Paige turned to Sorca, obviously as confused by the statement as Serath's bondmate.

"Not the bug," Eric said. "Aliens from one of the solar systems in the constellation Scorpii. They look like your standard movie Grays. And they can shapeshift."

"Grays are real?" Brendan's face actually lit up. So did Evelyn's.

Ari shook his head and Vay had turned ashen. She wove a little in place, as if she might topple over any moment.

Serath reached for Evelyn's hand and entwined their fingers, resting their arms on the table. He understood the danger of the situation.

"Scorpiians are assassins," he said. "They can take the form of any being whose DNA they've sampled. And they are nearly impossible to kill."

"The High Council uses them to collect bounties on individuals who are deemed extremely dangerous to the Coalition," Sorca said.

"I think it started out following me to try to get to Brendan." Eric spoke with confidence, even in such novel circumstances. Sorca's estimation of him increased yet again. "Probably due to his work on the communications array or his link to Kira."

"The Scorpiian changed targets after it learned that Eric had defeated me in combat," Sorca said.

"He... He what?" Khel leaned back in his chair, his eyes

wide as he stared at Eric.

Eric just shrugged. He smirked at Sorca. "Technically, the tree is what took you down."

"I refuse to be pair-bonded to a tree. And you're the one who spared my life instead of ending it. The victory is yours."

"Pair-bonded." Kira shook her head. "I don't understand."

"That makes a bunch of us, I think," Evelyn said.

Serath's scowl-creased brows formed a single dark line across his forehead. "Sorca is a Cygnian hybrid."

Kira glanced over with raised eyebrows. To her credit, she looked away quickly instead of indulging her curiosity with the long stares Sorca was more accustomed to when her true nature was revealed.

"Anybody want to clue the Earthlings in on what that means?" Brendan said.

"The Cygnians are a warrior race," Khel said. "Their prowess is legendary. They have incredible strength, skin like stone, and can—"

"Enough." Serath's booming voice made everyone jump in their seats. Evelyn grasped his arm in what Sorca now recognized as a reassuring gesture. He looked at Kira. "Explain."

After a few moments of silence, Kira spoke in an even voice. "Cygnian DNA is highly sought after by Coalition geneticists. The Cygnians consider any hybrids created to be their citizens. Part of the agreement in supplying us with their DNA is that the Coalition respect their customs."

"Okay," Brendan said. "So, how does that make them married?"

"Cygnians pair-bond through martial challenges," Kira added.

Brendan and Evelyn both said, "Oh," at the same time. Paige merely shook her head and smirked.

"Sorca has officially logged Eric as the victor in his challenge," Serath said. "The Coalition has no choice but to recognize their partnership. To do otherwise risks losing the cooperation of all the Cygnians among us and destroying relations between Cygnus-1 and the High Council."

The strain in his voice tugged at Sorca's heart in a way she wasn't sure she'd have been capable of even a day ago. Serath was the closest thing to a friend that she'd ever had. She didn't like the thought of bringing him difficulty or… pain. From the look on his face, perhaps he felt the same way about her and didn't want to see her leave his command for personal reasons, as well as due to his station.

"It is not yet certain whether I will relinquish my position," she said. "Eric will decide—"

"Excuse me." Eric leaned forward in his chair so that he could crane his neck around and hold her gaze. "*We* will decide. I'm not making any of these decisions alone. We're partners, remember?"

She smiled at him and nodded. Warmth flooded her

chest. It was so strange to not see herself as a tool.

She hoped Serath would understand. Victory in combat or not, she *wanted* Eric.

"I am...pleased to see that you have partnered with someone who shows you such respect," Serath said. "We will all need to support each other if we are to navigate the future successfully for Earth and the people of the Coalition."

The "people" of the Coalition? Not the Coalition itself. Sorca sat up straighter.

She had served with Serath for decades. She knew how he thought—or at least, she *had* known. Before he went to Earth and came back changed.

Was Serath planning on challenging the High Council? If so, she wanted to be part of that. Very, very badly.

"The Tau Ceti have access to new technology that threatens every sentient in the galaxy," Serath said. "We need to determine the source of this technology. There are also issues we need to address with the High Council, and even more that remains to be done on Earth."

"Brendan and I are ready to assist, sir," Kira said.

The corner of Serath's mouth twitched up for a brief moment. "I'm glad to hear it. You have quite a bit of work ahead of you. In light of Sorca and Eric's revelations, we will need to leave a larger contingent on Earth. The problem is more widespread than we originally estimated."

"Thank you, sir," Kira said.

Serath turned to Sorca, his glare back in full force. "Who will remain?"

"Vay, Ari, and Rin, for a start," Sorca said.

Vay's smile seemed to brighten the room even more than the lighting panels. Sorca had never seen someone look so excited. Ari leaned forward, as if he was about to argue, but then he let out a sigh and remained silent. Sorca doubted her next suggestion would pass without argument.

"And Khel," she said.

She didn't want to separate Khel and Paige. But if he and Sorca both remained on Earth, that would mean that Serath would lose both of his top officers in one reassignment.

"Khel and Paige are coming with the *Arbiter*," Serath said. "They've logged their pair-bond to enable her to join us and assist with our petition to the High Council for official recognition of Earth's first contact committee."

"Um, Department of Homeworld Security," Brendan said.

Serath let out a sigh, but went on. "I'll need a list of names. At least a dozen."

"A dozen?" Sorca couldn't hide her surprise. Serath was allocating an unusual amount of resources to Earth.

"I considered it a cultural exchange as well as a military assignment. Paige has expressed interest in helping planets who over-allocated their resources when they joined the Coalition," Serath said. "If she can help to increase their autonomy, it will decrease their burden on the Coalition."

"Are you sure the High Council actually wants that?" Eric said. "They seem pretty keen on keeping everyone under their control."

"We can only present our case," Serath said. "Much will be determined by their…reaction."

Sorca had a feeling he wasn't only thinking of the High Council giving new orders. If they ruled against Earth, how far was Serath willing to go to protect his bondmate's homeworld?

"Being pair-bonded to Sorca…" Eric said. "Does that mean I can join you as well when you present your petition to the High Council?"

Serath nodded. "It can be arranged."

Eric turned to Sorca, grasping her hand under the table and squeezing it. "We can be there and see their reaction ourselves. I want to meet the people who hold the fate of my world in their hands. Are you okay with that?"

"Yes."

"Sorca, think about this for a minute. What do *you* really want?"

She had never in her many lives been asked that question before Eric. The answer was as clear as the feelings growing in her heart for this amazing Earthling.

"It's what I want, too. I want to help your planet, and to fight for it by your side. And…I want to help my own people. They need to understand that they don't have to keep living this way."

She turned back to Serath and smiled. "Our attempts to change our culture will very likely get all of us killed. But we'll die in good company."

"And on that cheery note…" Brendan said.

"We're going to make it." Evelyn spoke calmly—her voice quiet, but stronger than Sorca had ever heard it. "The fate of our homeworld and the entire the galaxy is at stake. We'll succeed. We have to."

"Then we have our orders, from Serath's bondmate herself." Sorca lifted her arms over her head, dragging Eric's up with hers. "Victory!"

"What the hell." Eric shook his head, then yelled, "Victory!"

She grinned broadly.

This was going to be fun.

Epilogue

Sorca had pair-bonded. Vay still couldn't believe it, even after reading the entry five times. Sorca had logged the challenge in the official database for the Coalition of Planets, as well as the victory of Eric Peterson. There was no legal way around it.

First General Serath—now known as Adam Smith—had pair-bonded with Evelyn Chambers. Then the new planetary liaison, Kira, had logged her pair-bond with Brendan Sloan, the Earthling who'd formed the Department of Homeworld Security. And even Khel, the last Sadirian Vay would have ever thought capable of forming an emotional attachment to another, had fallen in love.

She shouldn't get her hopes up, but…

"What is it about this world?" Vay stared up at her monitor, the blue and white planet slowly spinning below, oblivious to its power over her people.

The Coalition was a virus. A blight on the free will of the galaxy. It devoured entire planets' resources, destroyed their cultures, and for what? The promise of technology that would extend sentient beings' lives and protect them from physical suffering, all the while drugging them into happiness and forcing them to spend their longer years in servitude?

A workstation behind her pinged and Vay jumped in her seat. She plastered a smile on her face as she glanced all around the empty room, even though she knew she was alone.

Nothing to see here. Just doing my job...

Thank the stars that the Coalition couldn't read minds. Yet. Vay at least had that last freedom—her own thoughts.

Still, she needed to be careful.

Earth had a strange potential. Humans were changing her people, and Sadirians hadn't really changed for thousands of years.

Vay wished she could get a closer look. She needed to talk to Earthlings, to figure out what they were doing that was having such a profound impact. If she could understand it, maybe she could leverage it to make some *real* change. Change beyond one ship, one crew.

With the help of Earth, they could change the galaxy. If she could find like-minded people who would help her, they could set everyone free.

She knew she shouldn't get her hopes up. But it was too late for that.

Staring intently at the blue planet in her view screen, she smiled again. A real smile this time.

"I *will* figure you out," she said.

Cassandra Chandler

—

That Scorpiian isn't done with the Department of Homeworld Security yet. It would be great if a tough Coalition soldier like Ari could get the drop on it—but that would be too easy. Enter Vay, the very combat-inexperienced cultural programmer assigned by General Serath, aka Adam Smith, to help everyone learn to get along. Don't worry, Vay. I believe in you. Read on for a sneak peek at *Entry Visa!*

Entry Visa

The Department of Homeworld Security
Book Five

Chapter One

"This is crazy." Vay repeated the statement as she walked toward the office of Earth's new planetary liaison, K-58-b7. Or, more simply, Kira.

Kira's bondmate, Brendan, stepped into the hallway. Vay quickly plastered a smile on her face. Hopefully, he hadn't heard her talking to herself.

"Hey, Vay." He used the same rhyming greeting every

time they interacted.

"Hey, Brendan. Is Kira in her office?"

"You're in luck. She just returned from the Himalayas." His ever-present smile widened. "I still can't believe you can get from Asia to Montana in half an hour."

"Coalition shuttles are a good bit faster than anything you've developed on Earth," Vay said.

He chuckled. "Maybe a little."

She grinned, happy he was playing along with her understatement. "Is she alone?"

"Yeah. She dropped off Ari and Rin to look for the Centaurans. We may finally have a lead on where their base is located."

"Centaurans don't have bases. They're nomadic, even on their own homeworld."

"No wonder we're having trouble finding them. Kira's lucky Adam left you behind to help out with the search."

"Thanks, but I don't think he was actually planning for me to help hunt down the rogue sentients invading Earth. Having a cultural programmer around was probably more about setting up Earth's First Contact committee."

Brendan arched an eyebrow at her.

"Oh, right," she said. "I mean, 'Department of Homeworld Security'."

He stepped around her, walking backward up the hall so that he could maintain eye contact. "See, that's what I like about you, Vay. You respect our culture."

"That's what I'm here for." Vay turned as well and took a few steps backward, trying to mirror his motions, but bumped into a table. She twisted quickly and managed to catch a vase that had started to tip toward the floor.

Brendan chuckled. "See you at dinner."

"Yeah." Vay cautiously stepped away from the table as he disappeared down the stairs at the end of the hall. "Maybe."

Hopefully not.

Her stomach was churning. What was she doing? She wasn't a soldier like the others. Okay, technically, they were all soldiers in the great fleet of the Coalition of Planets, but she was a scientist. A cultural programmer— one of the lowest ranking, most often denigrated positions in their entire society.

On a professional level, she found her fellow sentients' dismissal of her function fascinating. On a personal level, it "sucked ass", as Brendan would say.

The populations of new planets adapted to the Coalition's ways when they joined. It was mandatory. The only exceptions were the sentients who were physically incapable of imitating the dominant culture. And, if she was honest with herself, nobody in power cared about them.

The only Sadirians who cared about other cultures were the cultural programmers. And their job was supposed to be making life easier for the High Council and others in positions of power, not help the people being ruled.

"Why is this Antarean clicking at me? Is it an insult?"

"No, sir, that's just the noise their mandibles make when they're trying to form sounds in our language."

She was a facilitator, not a hunter. But Kira had limited resources, which presented Vay with an opportunity that she couldn't let pass by. She walked down the hallway with a more determined stride—being careful not to bump into any more furniture.

The door to Kira's office was open. Vay's heartbeat sped up. She had hoped she would have a few moments to build up her nerve to make her request, but Kira had probably heard her approach a mile away.

It was just an assignment—one that Vay desperately wanted. There was no harm in asking. Right?

"Are you just going to lurk in the hallway all day?"

Vay jumped at the low, strong voice echoing down the hall. There was no more time to second-guess herself. She quickly entered the office, hoping to appear confident instead of unprepared.

"Hi," Vay said. "I would ask how you heard me, but you did spend all that time running 'listening' stations." She made air-quotes around the word, the way Brendan had taught her.

Kira quirked up an eyebrow at the joke. And was that a hint of a smile?

Her dark hair was pulled back in a disheveled ponytail and there was a faint, yet distinct flush to her tanned skin.

But then, Brendan had just been visiting, and Vay doubted he would have left without a kiss.

A strong pulse of excitement shot through her system at her own memory—a single kiss shared with a special Earthling on Christmas Eve that had changed Vay's world forever.

Suddenly fortified, she said, "I wanted to talk to you about the signal we detected today."

"What about it?"

"It's really close. Minutes away by shuttle. It's weak and didn't last more than a few seconds, but I think we should still investigate it."

"Yes, and if I had anyone to send, I'd have already—"

"Send me."

Kira's eyebrows shot up on her forehead. "You?"

"I can handle it. Like I said, it's only minutes away. It's probably nothing. A small-time operation or maybe just a signal that escaped from a sentient passing through that area."

"What if it's the Scorpiian bounty hunter that we know is operating on Earth? We still haven't tracked it down."

"I can send a distress call."

"You wouldn't get a chance. You'd never see it coming." The determined gleam that seemed to live in Kira's eyes was back. Vay felt her opportunity slipping away.

"It's probably nothing," Vay said.

"But it *could* be something."

Desperate, she reached for any way she could reassure Kira enough to send Vay to investigate. "A Scorpiian wouldn't have made the mistake of letting a signal be detected."

"No one is perfect. And even if the signal is from another rogue sentient, the Scorpiian might have picked up on it and be headed there to hunt whatever bounty is on the trespasser."

"Which makes it all the more important that we act quickly. We can track it down and—"

"There are too many unknowns." Kira shook her head. "Of all the assignments I've given out so far, this is the most dangerous. It makes more sense to wait and send Ari."

"I've received the same training, even if my skill set was weighted toward more diplomatic resolutions. Maybe that will work in my favor."

"Scorpiians aren't known for their love of diplomacy. They're more known for their ability to conceal themselves, get close to their targets, and kill them."

"I'm aware of that, sir. I also know that Scorpiians blend in to reach their targets, stalking and studying them so they can fool even the closest of friends. They don't just murder anyone who gets in their way—it would bring too much attention to them. And they wouldn't make the mistake of letting a signal like this slip through, no matter how faint it is. Like you said in this morning's meeting, it's likely just a false alarm. Why wait and send Ari to confirm that, when you can send me now?"

"What if it *is* the Scorpiian and it isn't following their standard cultural protocols? What if it's not a false alarm?"

"Then I'll gather intel—from my ship, flying cloaked and at night—and let you know what's going on. I can run passive scans during the day while my ship is safely hidden in the forest of the region. And if it is a Scorpiian, I'll turn around and come back here immediately. It'll never see me leaving."

Kira snorted. "You've been spending too much time with Brendan. His sense of humor is rubbing off on you." She fixed her dark eyes on Vay, all sense of amusement vanishing. "Why is this so important to you? Really?"

"I can't say, sir. But it is important to me. I've studied Earth customs enough to walk among them if necessary. I can be there and back in a couple of days."

"Vay, if this is about how many of us have pair-bonded with humans—"

She laughed. "I can honestly say that I'm not asking for this assignment in the hopes that I'll run into an Earthling and feel some sort of magical connection that I'm compelled to act on, falling hopelessly in love."

It was true. Because that had already happened. With a tall, somewhat gangly, brown-haired, brown-eyed Earthling.

Henry had the greatest smile. He'd made Vay laugh, even when she could tell that he'd been dealing with something that weighed on him. And he'd shared something of himself with her—the ways of his people, and his own kin. He'd made her feel part of something beautiful and special.

She hadn't had a chance to ask him what was bothering him at the time. Ari had been waiting for her in a shuttle nearby. They weren't supposed to make the stop, but she'd been drawn to the festive lights decorating the small town and wanted to understand what was happening.

Luckily, Kira had been forgiving of the little side-trip, especially when Vay spun it as a cultural observation submission. And it seemed luck was helping Vay out again. Henry lived very close to the signal's origin.

He'd given her his phone number. She could use that to triangulate his position. Maybe she could see him again, even just one more time. But only if she received the assignment.

Vay did her best not to fidget under Kira's intense stare. After a few more moments, Kira shook her head.

"Go. Report in every hour when you're not in your rest cycle."

Vay was stunned. Was she really being allowed to go?

"Standard procedure is every three hours."

Kira raised an eyebrow at her.

"But I'll report in every hour," Vay said. "Yes, sir. Thank you, sir."

She turned and practically ran from the room before

Kira could change her mind.

—

About the Author

USA Today Bestselling author Cassandra Chandler uses her vivid imagination to make the world more interesting, spawning the ideas she turns into her whimsical Science Fiction romcoms and darkly evocative Paranormal and Urban Fantasy Romances. Fast-paced and funny, lighthearted or dark, her stories will introduce you to characters you want to be friends with and worlds where you'd like to build a vacation home.